QUOTATIONS FROM OTHER LIVES

# Quotations from Other Lives

## Stories by
## Penelope Gilliatt

Coward, McCann & Geoghegan
New York

Of the twelve stories in this book, eight appeared originally in *The New Yorker*.
"Twice Lucky" appeared originally in *The Observer Magazine*. "Fakt" appeared
originally in the *Sunday Telegraph Magazine*. "We're Here" appeared originally in
*British Vogue*. "When Are You Going Back?" appeared originally in *Encounter*. The
author is grateful to the publishers for their permission to publish in book form.
P. G.

Library of Congress Cataloging in Publication Data

Gilliatt, Penelope.
  Quotations from other lives.

  Contents: Break—Stephanie, Stephen, Steph,
Steve—Teeth—When are you going back?—[etc.]
  I. Title.
PR6057.I58Q6  1982    823'.914    81-19544
ISBN 0-698-11135-4              AACR2

*for Hugh Casson*

# Contents

# Break

ALASTAIR BROWN'S Scots ancestors had leapt over the Roman Wall to the North of England many centuries ago, but his later ancestors must have been as restless there as in Scotland, for in the fifteenth century a line of them had fled to what is now Czechoslovakia. Alastair, a Czech child in the nineteen-thirties times of anti-Semitism, had extremely formally told his family and friends that he was now to be called Eli. He wished to belong.

He was brought up in the castle of his grandfather, a Prague judge. Alert for hours after being put to bed, Eli lived in hope of hearing the sound of his grandfather's slippers on the stone corridors as the old man, who was unflawed in blitheness during the daytime, gave in to the beleaguered circumstances of his adopted country when the evening drew on. Eli would hear him dragging his bed from room to room, looking for somewhere to rest. Any room, anywhere. A man's world is carried with him. The old man's bed would be laden with books, and his cat would always follow him, wrecking the possibility of sleep by interestedly scratching pages to bits. From the cat's point of view, this nightly adventure was another day, and hurrah for that. Anything for activity. From the cat's point of view, again, there was no such thing as an appointed time for a party or for breakfast.

This dorm feast of paper and company represented both. The old man understood that. Tired, though, and in spite of being ashamed of himself, he would flick the infernal engrossed animal off his books. Then his conscience smote him, of course, and he would take the cat down to the old prison of the castle, which had once been a trial house; the jail was now the kitchen, and the judge would feed the cat.

Eli had heard of all this. He was shipped off from Prague as a schoolboy, for safety. He went to America. It seemed a way out. He learned Villon's French, Latin, and Hebrew. In New York, he felt among kin. On Broadway, especially, the place where many people are to be heard muttering to themselves in many languages. Then, when he had crossed the Atlantic again, thoughts of his grandfather's profession took him to Oxford to read Modern Greats and Law. He practiced law until his forties, when he more and more pressingly understood that his knowledge of civil law was doing his clients less and less good. A poor man would come to him with a case. This apple tree, you see. It was growing in this man's back garden; had been for eighty years. But now it was drooping over the wall into a neighbor's garden, and the neighbor was a wretch who never returned so much as a lent cupful of flour; and, besides that, the apples were dropping into his neighbor's garden. So whom did the apples belong to? Could Eli get the apples, because the man wanted them for his adopted son, who, being West Indian, had never had the pleasure of apple snow and apple queen's cake and apple pie? Eli would give his best advice. But sometimes even he would lose the case. Paying mind to such clients, he found their toll in hope and time too much. He made a decision to go back to America and learn there to be a doctor. When he had made the decision, he leaned his head against the cold wall over the drawing-room fireplace and sobbed, as men will when decisions have been made.

He put on a Fred Astaire album to cheer himself. His daily came into the room—his nightly, rather, for she was the one who cooked for him when he came back from chambers—and danced with him. Things bettered. They danced until two in the morning. Eli started to play the piano and then the maid danced by herself. A pretty woman, small, the shape of a yellowhammer with its feathers plumped out against the cold, but she danced lightly. It is often said of the plump that they are cumbersome, but it seems to be more of a truth that they are dainty. More often the thin are landlocked and blunder into things.

"You'll have noticed, sir," she said, dancing a foxtrot with herself as he played, "that the ironmongers came today. They said that they had come to see the fireplace. That they had come to take away the guard. I thought they said they had come to take away God, but after a sec I recollected myself and I said to myself, 'Nora, you're not a God-fearing woman.'"

"It's all right now," he said, playing "By Myself." "'I'll go my way by myself,'" he sang. "'I'm by myself alone.' I don't know why people always say that this is a man's tune."

So Eli came back to New York, and took a medical degree. Another discipline. It was, of course, late in life, but there are always further chances, he would say to himself at night. He had come across the Atlantic by ship, because of the weight of his luggage. He wanted all his books with him. They were now in his quite grand-looking office: many of them old Penguins and rare copies, in wartime utility paper, of Eliot, Auden, Spender ("One bullet in ten thousand kills a man"), Stevie Smith, Kafka, Edward Lear (the Indian drawings), P. G. Wodehouse, C. S. Lewis, Beckett in French. Few patients noticed them, or the tattered series of "New Writing," though one would have thought them apparent among the medical tomes.

Eli was poor and slept on a camp bed in his waiting room to save rent. Folly for a single man to pay double rent. His office had a bathroom. He did without secretary or nurse and spent the weekend paying bills and sending out his own, these last often not even acknowledged. He retained scorn of the employees of bill-collection businesses, being his own man, though he knew his present life to be one of attrition and his lack of any way of cooking for his friends to be meager-spirited.

"'AN interlude,'" Eli said to himself. "'Lear.'" And some Perrier while he thought. For the sake of its being European, though this thing called Canada Dry Club Soda was cheaper. But where was the club?

He always kept his passport renewed. Exits important. Cleave to choice. He addressed his waiting room. "The point of this lonely place is that it possibly holds out hope of being a good place to look for a good place from."

AND at the same time, in the same land, in the same city, a countrywoman of his called Averil Paget was playing tennis of a sort in a playground with her daughter, Eliza. Eliza, being seven, had a short-handled racquet. Averil made a gentle serve to her, underhand, from four feet away, and Eliza missed it. Averil made a dive to stop the ongoing ball from hitting a toddler in the face, saved the ball, and tore a calf muscle. She went across the street to her apartment on her hands and knees, with Eliza on her back. To Eliza it seemed play, and to Averil on hands and knees the calf muscle gave no hurt. The street was a street so enlightened that it had, by block occupants' wish, been improved to the extent that no fire engines or ambulances could get in, the entrance and the exit having been so inefficiently narrowed—artistically narrowed—that barely a skateboard got in past the parked cars. This artistic element had come into things through hope of giving the impression of a slightly European mall. There were also, for the same aesthetic reasons, and by block vote, large figurative concrete ducks beside each lamp-post and fire hydrant. Two men were in the street digging up the electrical wires and the telephone wires: respectively, Averil trusted. They looked with admiration at the sight of a pretty young mother giving her daughter a treat by riding her on her grownup hands and knees.

Averil made it up the five steps to the front door, on hands and knees. Eliza used the keys, because Averil couldn't reach. They went in, Eliza carefully leading.

Eliza, listening hard for what was to happen next, heard her mother on the telephone asking four friends how to find a doctor. It was, of course, a Sunday, but Dr. Eli Brown would be in, said one of Averil's best friends, Michele. Dr. Brown, she said, was always in on Sunday mornings doing the bills.

"Dr. Brown, I think I've broken a plantaris muscle," Averil said on the telephone.

"Which leg does it appear to be?"

"It is quite definitely the right. I mean, I can feel it, you see."

"And what makes you think it is the plantaris muscle?"

"I shouldn't have said 'I think.' I *know* it's the plantaris muscle."

"How do you know?"

"Because I've done it before."

"I'd have to see you."

"Yes, of course."

Eliza brought her a ginger ale and the bottle opener, not yet being able to use a bottle opener.

"And when did you do it before?" said Dr. Eli Brown.

"When I was skiing."

"The plantaris muscle is a useless muscle. It doesn't do any work for us."

"No, I know, but it's stopping my being able to walk."

"Is the pain like being hit in the calf by a very hard serve from a tennis ball?"

"I hadn't thought of it that way, but roughly."

"Roughly?"

"In this case, I was playing tennis with my daughter in a playground and the ball was going toward her from the front. From me to her, you see. So I didn't feel any tennis ball on the back of my leg. My particular leg."

"We'd better see you. I'm on my own. It's not easy on a Sunday, but we'll manage somehow."

Why "we"?

And Averil also pondered "somehow." There was no grownup in the house to help, and she would have to drive to the doctor herself, with Eliza. Every nearby friend was out by now, and Dr. Brown's bills pressed. Averil crawled down the steps again, and Eliza, comforted by their alliance in such circumstances, equipped the car's glove compartment with more bottles of ginger ale and some toffees. Averil, who owned a sports Volvo, drove it on the gear stick and the hand brake and the hand throttle, keeping the leg that worked for the clutch. Parking was no difficulty.

The doctor's office was at the end of a wide and long marble passage watched by two liveried doormen, who were obviously bewildered by the sight of a woman on hands and knees and didn't catch the idea that a manly shoulder or two would make a deal of difference.

Eliza ran up to Dr. Brown, who was standing at the top of six stairs leading into his office, and said, "She's coming."

"Take your time," shouted Dr. Brown to Averil.

DR. BROWN, nurseless and secretaryless, took unnecessary details for billing, very slowly, on an electric typewriter.

"It keeps hitting me when I tell it to get to the next line," he said.

"I know. and when you're not using it, it makes that reproachful hum. Do you want me to help?"

He looked around at her sympathetic position, which hurt her. Then, locked again into his thin frame, he continued: from a skyless cell, it seemed. He wanted Averil's name, address, age, marital status, medical history ("chicken pox"), and he put in "possible case of repeated ruptured right plantaris muscle." "Billing address" had to be where she lived ("resided") in New York, not where she worked. "Credit information nil," he typed, very slowly; and then, looking at her over his spectacles, "You don't use charge cards?"

"I'm afraid not."

"Nor do I. Now we'll climb onto the couch. No, not that way. Up the steps."

"Eliza, darling, I saw some magazines in the doctor's waiting room." Eliza looked back as she left, unwilling to go.

"You see, Dr. Brown, I can't get up the steps, because of this leg. I can get up backward right onto the bed if you'll be patient."

But he was kind. He gave Eliza diversions, outside in the waiting room.

"Are you all right? How are you feeling?" he asked Averil when he came back in. "What are you laughing about?"

"I was thinking that the last time I asked somebody that question about 'How are you,' he said, and it took a long time, 'Well, you see, I've got these two colds. One coming and one going.'"

Dr. Brown tried to grow serious and said, "Yes, I'm afraid we've got a ruptured plantaris here. Six weeks. A cast. What are you laughing about now?"

"Perhaps there's something peculiar about me."

"Do you feel the need of an aspirin?"

"No. I mean, no, thank you."

Eliza came in, gave toffees to all three of them, and then, bored, went back to the waiting room to tear things out of the *National Geographic.*

"While we're sitting around for the plaster to dry, what were you laughing about that time?" asked the doctor.

"Only that my little girl, who's wrecking your magazines—"

"It doesn't matter—"

"—that she brought across with us in the car some English

newspapers that are in the middle of a circulation battle, and one that I'm particularly fond of had the headline GLOOM SPREADS."

"It doesn't in you, does it?" said Dr. Brown.

"The last time this muscle thing happened, the doctor kept on telling me it was going to make me cry for six weeks and that he didn't tell men patients that but he was telling me because women are more used to putting up with pain. Are they?"

"It seems to me that they try. People do. Your daughter is trying to do something that is beyond her, and she's doing it." Dr. Brown tested the plaster. "Did it?"

"Did it what?"

"Make you cry for six weeks?"

"No."

Dr. Brown nodded.

"I was wondering whether women are used to putting up with things. I'm going to ask you again," said Averil.

"I don't think so, do you? Used, perhaps, but not inured."

DR. BROWN saw her downstairs. Carried her piggyback. Eliza was delighted. He sent no bill. Every four days he rang up to find out how she was managing to get to work after taking Eliza to school. Many another day Michele, the friend who had recommended Dr. Eli Brown, would ring up and ask if there was anything she could do to help. This struck Averil as being most good of her, as Michele was badly off, though learned, and living a long way away by bus; twice she turned up with books and honey.

Dr. Brown came to Averil's house one evening to see how she was. Working, reading. Eliza in bed. He had brought with him a headline for Averil. KNIGHT'S NEPHEW UNINJURED. After begging to be excused for intruding, in a Russian manner, he took off his muffler and his hat, holding them in his hand.

"Pardon me," he said. "How is the leg?"

She had had it up on the diningroom table. "The cast makes things a bit difficult."

He took off the cast, with heed, and she walked fast around the room.

"You walk on the balls of your feet, like a ballet dancer," he said.

"Apparently I always have."

"For a time, wear high heels."

"What a doctor, to say something like that. One of the greatest friends I have ever had, rather a poor man who plods around in tennis shoes, but a man of distinction—no, of distinctiveness—gave me a voucher last Christmas for a great deal of money to buy two pairs of shoes at the shoe shop he knew I had always gone to in London and Paris."

Still walking on the balls of her feet, liberated and gay, she made some very strong black coffee of the kind she liked.

"Great," he said. "Costly?"

"Tuppence halfpenny in this part of New York. Spaniards and Italians and Russians all around."

"Tuppence halfpenny, you said. But you've moved on to the decimal system."

"It's an expression, you see. Expressions don't die out in old countries, as long as the language goes on leaving room for new ones. Inventing them."

"I noticed once that you used the word 'gubbins.' Could we look it up?"

"I don't think it would be in any dictionary yet. I just happened to use it. It means, oh, say, nonsense, trivia, nothing to get het up about. I particularly like a word that has the sound of Anglo-Saxon in it. I don't go much for Latinate words, do you?"

"You sound as if you're offering me a piece of cake that you hate but that you don't want to throw out."

"Latinate words are the ones that won't shut up, but I suppose they carry on to some purpose to someone."

"Go on walking about. Superior. Yes. And forgive me, but

you also look very pretty. What discussion are you and your daughter engaged in at the moment? I notice that you talk to each other a good deal."

"She's been teaching me about a game called D. and D. It's played with dice. The initials stand for Dungeons and Dragons. I don't understand the rules properly, partly because it seems that the rules alter from place to place and group to group. Each child rolls the dice to give him intellect, bravery, wisdom, charisma, health, or ingenuity. She didn't mention looks. I asked her whether anyone was cursed with evil qualities like cowardice, but they're not. The point is that the children are at the mercy of the Dungeons and the Dragons, and all the children are in alliance. No player is an enemy. The enemy can't be seen. The children I've talked to can't define it. You see, it's a child's position, isn't it. Unseen enemy, no rules, concrete possessions their only protection. The dice aren't talismans."

Dr. Brown poured her some coffee and she drank it back in a gulp as if she were a Slav and it slivovitz.

"Is the enemy the grownup world?" she said. "In the sense that it's been allotted to them? Nothing they can do about it."

"The game." He sneezed. "I suppose I sneezed because I was going to say something about talismans."

"Gesundheit and serves you right. Good grief, a doctor talking about talismans."

The doctor put her skinny leg onto a chair but she said it was fine and made them some more coffee.

Leaning forward, she said, "It struck me that that was a pretty good game. Having all the players in concord. All being in danger but not knowing the rules. A fight to the death without referee, though there is nothing but a gang of friends visible. It's interesting."

Later on that evening, they spoke of his life as it had been spent early on in Czechoslovakia. They talked for many other evenings. They lived together. When it came to their wedding, Averil asked Michele to be a witness.

"Darling," said Michele on the telephone, "you're getting married to Dr. Brown?"

"Yes. You said he might be harsh because you don't trust men under a hundred and whatever-it-was pounds, but he's not at all. Harsh. When he left Czechoslovakia at twelve, his only worldly goods were the gold fillings in his mouth."

"His?"

"Dr. Brown's."

"Ellie Brown's?"

"You said Eli Brown."

"You said you were getting married to Ellie Brown? Didn't you look her up in the directory? Granted that she's under a hundred and whatever pounds and is indeed a bit harsh—"

"But he's not harsh."

"All right. He. But didn't you look him up in the directory and check that he wasn't the she I'd told you to go to?"

"The address seemed all right and he's a he and there we are."

"Who did you say had recommended you? Did you mention any other patients?"

"He kept looking them up in *Who Was Who* and I said I thought that was glum for him, and he said he thought I was suffering more than I was saying from this fatuous muscle and that a cast would put it right in six weeks. And even if he's the wrong doctor by your lights, a piece of good fortune has come our way. Of luck." She stopped, as other people do on the telephone when they are lighting a cigarette, and Michele waited, knowing that she didn't smoke. "Good word, 'luck.' Words to be saved. Girl, gay, blithe, swink. All monosyllables, you see. Interesting that the word 'spondee' describes its meaning within its sound, but that five-syllable 'mono-syllable' goes on and on."

"'Swink' being?"

"'Toil.'"

# Stephanie, Stephen, Steph, Steve

SHE had been christened in 1929. Stephanie Angelica Bysshe Talbot, with the surname of Duncan, at the Cumberland family seat. One of the family seats. There were three. Her mother was also named Stephanie, it having been laid down by her overbearing great-great-grandfather Stephen, on her father's side, in his will, that any and all descendants and descendants' spouses or beneficiaries were to be christened, or to adopt the name by deed poll, Stephen or Stephanie, in honor of the aforesaid Stephen's repute and his fortune.

And as to these three family seats, the baby Stephanie's mother, Stephanie, had been saying to her husband for a long time that she wished a fraction of this withering fortune could be spent on chairs designed for sitting without bruises, adapted to reading, or writing, or thinking.

"A total of two hundred and seventy-one Cromwellian studded-leather chairs in three counties cries out for a few reading chairs, doesn't it? Upholstered, possibly? Some cushions?"

"The places were not originally architected to be originally furnished that way."

"But originally was a long time ago, seen from now. It isn't as though we had roast swan for dinner every night."

"I don't see how such things as you suggest would fit in."

"We could make at least one room *possible* to live in.

Without offense to the rest of the house. Couldn't we?"

"I don't see how."

Seats and chairs. Stephanie drove into the market town and bought six deck chairs. Visibly glad that Stephanie had made the move, Stephen even liked the chairs' canvas.

"I haven't ever seen canvas before, except as sails. Interesting. I must say you look much more comfortable now. Stephanie, you *are* much more comfortable?"

"Yes, much. I don't suppose one's ever exactly comfortable when one's eight months pregnant."

"You've made the room very pretty." He looked round again at the room: the yellow cushions, his wife in muslin reading, the white voile curtains blowing. He touched one of the curtains, thinking not to be seen, and she laughed and said, "That was like the business with hugging the bookcase in Chekhov. The curtains are made of nearly the same stuff as my dress." She held out her hands. "You *could* even touch the dress." He was not then alert to irony, but she remembered that he had once said—later apologizing—"When you hug me you hurt me."

"There are some chocs over there," she said: she making time, and he glad of it. He brought them and said quickly, "I've got to go away to the shipyard. Before that, I'm going to sail round the country. I shan't be here when the baby's born. And don't plead."

She stayed quiet.

"And don't hold your tongue."

"You've left out 'either.' You need it. Because of the contradiction," she said. Pause. "Don't worry. There'd be nothing you could do anyway, and births happen every minute, and I know it would be wretched for you not to be able to help. Let's play Truisms. The truisms that aren't true."

"The trouble is that we must have played them all by now."

"Stephen, let your mind wander. What about the dinner

party we had the night before last? That was fairly flush with them. 'The best things in life are free.'"

"That was said by the woman who'd inherited sixty-five million in tinned soups."

"'You can always tell a lady by her accessories.'"

He said quickly, pleased, "'You deserve the best.' It's the hallmark of stinginess."

"'New York isn't America.'"

"'It's not the heat, it's the humidity.'"

"Have you been seeing a lot of tropical people lately?"

"No, but one stores things up."

"This is one turned round the way it should be," said Stephen. "'When you've lain on your bed, you must make it.'"

"Yes," said Stephanie. "Well done. 'When people are angry they say a lot of things that they mean.' When are you leaving? I could tell it would be soon."

"Tomorrow."

WHEN the baby Stephanie was born, she had two tufts of bright red hair. They were the color that hair has turned on some of the skeletons in the crypt of St. Bride's. There are many clichés about the hope carried into a house by the newborn, but this one's character was different, and everyone who spent time with her saw it. She clearly already knew the dark side of life, though she was rapturous company from the start. Her mother foresaw in flashes the course of Stephanie's youth, prowess, age. In one dream she dreamed "Bankrupt of life, yet prodigal of ease." She woke, still thinking of Dryden, and looked at the baby in her cradle. She wrote a letter to Stephen saying that the baby was a girl and that, as she was going to have to be called Stephanie, her mamma was ready to answer to Steph if absolutely necessary, or to anything else except Stuffy, which her governess had called her before her adenoids were taken out. She had nowhere to send the letter except to the shipyard, where her husband was not due for two months. She died that night.

                              *      *      *

A FEW letters, necessarily without return addresses, arrived
from her husband during that time. Unemployment was
growing all over the North, but it took him a while to gather
the situation. Starting as he did from Land's End, he noticed
first the swing of the sardine harvest away from the coast of
Cornwall. He did what he could about the fishermen who
were out of luck. At poor times of night, when he was
incapable of saying to himself how much he missed Stephanie, he would stomp into the cabin of one or another of his
crew and bring out maps to get on with things, though once
he bawled, "I should be up there! Driven out of my own
house!" Then, of course, a difficult apology. First babies,
thought the crew, sleepy and resentful.

*A letter, 1929*

MY DARLING,
    Today—no, tonight, I can't sleep for my concern about
you—a St. Ives meeting about the sardines.
    Tomorrow we set off. Our itinerary will come to you as
soon as possible.
                                                             S.


*A letter, 1929*

MY DARLING,
    Sleep still impossible. A lot of fishermen still out of work,
though some moved to tin mining. Now: St. Clears, Car-
marthen, Llandovery, Trecastle, Brecon, Hay, Hereford (a
few miles further inland—nearer to you, my heart), the
Outer Hebrides, many other places you wouldn't know of,
no addresses of inns or pubs or digs to give you, so we *are* in
the dark, aren't we. I am sure you are looking as beautiful as
ever. Then I go to the shipyard. How I long to see you.
Would you be your usual sweet self and ask Mrs. Watson to
get in plenty of salted butter and a supply of potted shrimps

nearer arrival, because there will be quite a few of us and I know that would go down well? Have snatched some time from the tiller to write some of the poetry of mine that you like, though I remember being v. hurt by several literary experiments that you said were "pensive-couch department." You see how seriously I take your criticism. I trust you will be as rapt by these endeavors as I am; and how the baby will enjoy them. Any letters you have written, though we know writing isn't your forte, will best find me at the shipyard.

Again and again,
my dear love,
YOUR HUSBAND

*A letter, 1929*

MY DARLING,

High winds. Shall have this posted as soon as possible. I forgot to mention that the crew greatly likes beer, so Mrs. Watson should get in a goodly supply.

In haste,
YOUR HUSBAND

WHEN Stephen eventually reached his family shipyard on the Northeast Coast, he found two-thirds of the men laid off. He had had no idea of what the crisis could come to. He also found many letters from Stephanie, carefully dated, giving him newspaper cuttings and, at length, her own understanding of the national situation. She had the intent focus that he was later to find in his daughter. It was in her last letter that she had given him the news of the baby's birth. And then telegrams from Mrs. Watson and from the Cumberland doctor, telling him of Stephanie's death. His secretary, Mary, at the shipyard, still working but without income, had opened the telegrams and thought it best to put them on top of Stephanie's letters to him. He seemed to Mary to wish her to stay in his office for a while.

"We must do something about these office chairs, mustn't we," he said.

She made a note.

"I don't know what to do next. I mean what to do first."

She waited a long while indeed.

"Can we get hold of Mrs. Watson? I'm sorry, can *you*, and when you do I'll come in straightaway? I've got to go out for a breath of air." He lifted his spectacles and consulted her face in request, for the first time in their knowledge of each other. "You must have been working for months for no money," he said.

"There isn't any."

She got Mrs. Watson and then the doctor. As she heard Stephen speaking, he sounded so ice-cold that Mary found him a blanket and some hot water. In the deserted shipyard there was no chance of tea.

"Where are the other directors, Mary?"

"Down South. There's a certain hostility from the men, sir."

"There are some documents I need." Agreements, contracts, his own bank statements, his assets. He wrote a list. He telephoned the other directors to tell them what he was going to do. They disagreed violently with him. So he acted on his own. He telephoned the unions concerned. He spoke to them with liberty, and they agreed to call a mass meeting of the laid-off men the next day. In the night, in his office, it could be said that he had a crackup. From three to five was the worst time to get through. The men gathered without sense of purpose at seven-thirty or thereabouts. No point in being on time when there was no work. He thought that he wasn't an open speaker, but his character seemed to Mary much changed.

"Not much doing, is there? Well, there should be, and I've talked to the other directors, they're all down South, and I've talked to the unions, and we ask you to build a ship."

A voice from the crowd yelled, "What's she called?"

"*Talbot*," shouted Stephen. "H.M.S. *Talbot*. Who's willing? To get back to work at your proper wages?"

Another voice from the cloth-capped crowd: "Who's paying?"

Stephen: "Our company."

A ship engineer: "Bliddy company. Like enough *they'd* fork out. I'd eat my hat. You're the only bigwig who's shown his face at last. Know how much the dole is?"

Stephen gave the wretched amount. Though he didn't like separating himself from the directors who were making their way on the stock market down South, he came out with it: "I'm paying for this ship. The unions have your contracts, underwritten by me. You've got my word. You've turned up and I've turned up and I want you all to sign and you can stand me a pint when I'm broke. Who'll come in?"

The hands went up. Over three-quarters of the men.

Stephen went on: "Your contracts are in the office, with Mary and me. We want this ship by the end of the year."

A voice from the crowd: "You weren't here for two month, mate."

"See here," shouted Stephen. "We all turned up, didn't we?"

HAVING financed the ship from his own shares in the company and with much of his own fortune, Stephen was hardly a rich man any longer. He managed to keep his place in the company, though none of the other directors agreed with his compliance with the unions. He sold all three of the family seats, thinking often of Stephanie's wish for comfortable chairs and of her amicably combative presence. Living now in the West Lodge of the Cumberland house, lying in the double bed that he and Stephanie had so long shared, he had the docile hallucination that she was lying beside him. He got up quietly and shaved and made their breakfast. In the kitchen he thought of the bed, still the same, the yellow curtains she had wanted, the deck chairs. Even if they were in a minute cottage, nothing of consequence had changed, he thought. A man should shave before breakfast, and Stephanie should have breakfast in bed, he thought. He carried the breakfast up the small stairs. He talked to Mrs. Watson through her bedroom door and went into the nursery to whistle to the baby. Covering the tray with a pram blanket, he whistled bits of a Handel saraband and "Voi che sapete" and the mandolin song from *Don Giovanni*. But when he went into the big bedroom, no movement from the double bed. Still stirred by the force of his wish to meet obligations about which he knew himself to have been faulty, he looked at the grandfather clock that had been moved from the big house, found it telling 5:10; corrected his own watch that told 8:45, thinking that it had stopped the night before; and sat with the baby. At 6:15 by his newly set watch, Mrs. Watson came in to the small Stephanie. He picked up the breakfast tray for two and said to her, "I'm just going down to redo our boiled eggs and heat up our coffee."

"Coffee boiled is coffee spoiled, sir," she said, nodding, wondering what to do with this man out of his wits.

"Mrs. Duncan still asleep, Mrs. Watson."

"Yes, sir."

"Sleeping quite heavily. On the usual side of the bed, of course. Not that anything else is usual for the moment. But the ship's coming along. That's one thing." He took the breakfast tray back to the kitchen, timed two new boiled eggs, made new coffee, carried the renewed tray upstairs, and sat at the bottom of the hump in the bedclothes for a while, until he realized that the hump was on his side of the bed and marked where he had briefly slept that night. Stephanie's side of the bed was now quite flat. But she had been there all night with him, he felt sure. He thought for a long while, rang the local telephone operator for the time, reset the clock and his watch to the time the watch had been keeping in the first place. But he had been perfectly awake. The making of the breakfast had been no dream. A man gone bonkers wouldn't be able to time boiled eggs, would he? He ate one of the cooling eggs, then the second one, so as not to be faithless to such a powerfully rational tray. Even as he drove to the shipyard, still not late, he found it hard to believe that a reasonable man could make such a dark error. In a half-awake nightmare, possibly. But fully awake, and in daylight. At the shipyard, he telephoned Mrs. Watson and tried to be level, to ask her to clear away the breakfast tray, to say lightly that he had made a mistake, to ask about young Stephanie. He missed his wife more than ever. He used the word "hallucination" to himself with severe irony. "*I* should have washed the breakfast tray," he muttered to himself. "It can't be so. She must be there. I'm *not* bonkers." He thought, with his chin on his hands, and then signed a pile of checks that Mary had left for him in the folder marked "For signature today." Today being, presumably, today.

"Is today today?" he asked Mary, pulling down the points of his waistcoat.

"Yes, sir."

"And I haven't gone mad?"

"No, sir," she said, looking at the date on the checks he had signed.

"In that case, the folder you yesterday must have marked 'today' isn't very clear, is it? A dive into delirium, I should call it. Put the *date* on the folder in future, in pencil, then rub it out, and when you're writing 'today' on what will always be yesterday, put the *date* of the next today. Is that clear? Oh, and this folder about things to be done, which you call 'Bring back.' Apart from its sounding like a command to a dog about a bone, and you know I don't like dogs, I think you mean 'Bring *forward*.' The folder holds the things getting nearer to us. So it's obviously 'Bring forward.' Nearer to us." Angry with her for not being Stephanie and for being alive, he added, "It's a matter of asking for action *sooner*, don't you see? For movement *forward*. Not *later*, movement *away* from you. Unless the you is someone standing at the end of the time continuum? Look up 'continuum' in the *O.E.D.* if you don't know it."

"I only have a *Secretary's Friend.*" He looked at her minute dictionary, with its dolefully wrong information about subtleties and roots, and thought it no friend. In the shipyard's lunch hour he went out and bought her the two-volume *O.E.D.*

"It's called 'The Shorter,'" she said. "Shorter than what? It's huge. Oh dear, it would have been costly." She went to the office kitchen, saying "Thank you," and made him a cup of the deep-black coffee that he liked, from the freshly ground beans called Continental.

"The proper one, the plain *Oxford English Dictionary*, volumes and volumes of it, would be a weight to look things up in, I thought." He took the coffee and thanked her. "But I can picture you being very happy with the complete, so we can go a bust on it later as an office expense when there's anything coming in to put expenses against."

"You do cleave to the next thing, sir."

"I'm afraid I don't. This morning early I slithered downstairs and got a breakfast tray for Mrs. Duncan and me, because she was asleep in the bed beside me and I waited, and she wasn't. Wasn't there."

Mary read the dictionary. "Interesting word here, sir. 'Wanhope.' Why should it mean despair? It says 'archaic' anyway."

"What would it mean to you?"

"Hope despite everything." She had some of her own tea— very sweet, a blend that was free if you collected enough coupons—and said in the manner of a dictionary, "2. Fragile hope."

"As there's no reliable country address for me now, let's address everything from the shipyard. Even personal letters, you see. If I have to go down South, you'll open everything. Otherwise I'll be here every day as usual. But starting at twelve noon, because I want to see Stephanie in the mornings. The baby Stephanie."

*    *    *

STEPHEN employed a tutor for Stephanie when she was ten. The tutor, called Steve, which further complicated things, was just down from Oxford. Steve and Mrs. Watson got on, except that Mrs. Watson had trouble with his habit of asking her in to sherry at six-thirty each evening in his bedroom, heavy with the smell of his pipe.

"This room has a Scots mist of your tobacco, Steve. You don't seem able to read a book without smoking. There's a shaggy Highland-cattle stink about the place. Cumberland isn't Scotland, Steve."

"Your usual sherry? Let's choose another topic."

"Pardon?"

"At an Oxford tutorial one always agrees on a topic. Then one—oneself and one's tutor—talks about it."

Mrs. Watson smoothed her apron and felt young. She got up, using the bottom of Steve's bedstead as a ballet barre, and danced. High kicks, done facing away from him, because she wasn't dressed for it.

"You've got an extraordinary turnout," he said, responding. "I'd no idea."

"It's not my own. It's modeled on Jessie Matthews' in *Evergreen*. I think I could have been something of a star if I'd had enough of a mirror. You can't practice without a nice big mirror. Mrs. Duncan gave me one when she saw my interest. It must have cost the earth. But a bird got into my room and smashed it, and I wouldn't have asked for another. That being in the big house, of course. There wouldn't be room here anyway. So I do it in the bathroom and while I'm washing up. I got a biggish old mirror, and I prop it up under the sink so that I can put in an hour or two of work after dinner. Propped on the floor, you understand. An acrobat once said to me that he liked to work full figure."

"What are you drinking?" Steve asked when she had sat down.

"It's a port-and-lemon. I can't quite get on with your

sherry. It makes me feel fuzzy. Not that I'm not accustomed to wines. When I'm simmering a salmon, there's always two tablespoons of white cooking wine in the stock. I expect you'll have noticed."

"I thought it might be vinegar."

"It may have gone off. I'm not a taster. You see how a conversation can move? It doesn't need a push from your Oxford things. We've talked about smoking, Oxford, Jessie Matthews, mirrors, wine, and very pleasant it's been."

"What happened to Mr. Watson, if I may ask?"

"We were in service together. Nineteen twenty-one it would have been. I was a book learner then, like you and Stephanie." She drank some of her port-and-lemon. "One day, after the dinner, he came into the kitchen and found me reading a book. Very angry he was. Reading in front of the cook, me being a betweenmaid, you see. As butler is to bootboy, so is cook to betweenmaid."

"And what was the book?" Forgetfully, Steve filled another pipe.

"I was interested in women's rights, you know, and much taken by the sea. The book was rather narky about the idea of women seamen, being written in the last century, but you could put up with it. Always interesting to hear the other side. It was called *Let Them Be Sea Captains If They Will*.

"Unkind," said Steve.

"Well, I learned quite a bit. Knots, rigging. It wasn't the time when I could really have been a sea captain, so he'd got me in a way, but I can't complain. I can sail a three-masted schooner quite well, given a good crew."

"Really?"

"It's in the mind, you see. When I was Stephanie's age or a bit older, I used to rub the palms of my hands up and down tree trunks to make them rough. As if I'd been hauling on ropes. Of course, the dishwashing does it now."

"And Mr. Watson?"

"He left me that night. But that's not to say that his getting into a tantrum about my reading a book has put me against books. They don't necessarily lead to the end of a marriage. Where would you say young Stephanie was bound for?"

"I'm worried that she's lonely. A man's no company hour after hour for a girl of ten."

"Children are hard to come by in this part of the world. It's mostly sheep. And the big houses here and there, of course, but the owners all send their children to public schools down South. Well, we'll put our minds to it. There's a very nice little girl just her age in the fishmonger's. Would you say she liked boys yet?"

"She says all the boys she's ever met are rough. I shouldn't be surprised."

"There's a nice lad who's the son of our organist. At least, it's a harmonium, but I've heard him at the organ in the Abbey, so we've decided to collect for an organ for our church."

"Perhaps the organist could teach her. She seems interested in music, and who knows where it might lead."

DURING the Second World War, Mrs. Watson had to leave to work in munitions. Steve, being ill, was exempt. Stephanie regretted that she was too young to go into the Wrens. Perhaps the war would go on for years and years and the minimum age would get earlier. The shipyard was working at full speed. Stephen was so tired that he sometimes slept in the office. Ringing Stephanie whenever he was likely to be away overnight, he caught himself saying, "There's a hitch this end, so I may not quite be there. No, I may not totally be there." Stephanie laughed, not seeing the difference, and Stephen said, "Your mamma would have explained."

"That's the air-raid siren your end."

"It always goes about this time."

"I think I'd like to be with you."

Stephen considered that for a moment and then asked Steve to bring her to him by train, saving the rationed petrol.

She arrived and typed two short letters for him, with many mistakes, but dexterously. Though the carbon paper often went in backward, she would always begin again.

"You do that pretty fast," said Stephen, working at another desk.

"It's like scales."

"Do you like the organist?"

"Not much."

"Why?"

"He's so hairy. Also he makes jokes that aren't funny. How close was that last lot of bombs?"

"I should say about three miles. They missed what they wanted. The ships."

He took her home when the all-clear had gone, and set up a camp bed for her in the office. Again, disapproval from the other directors.

A battleship was lost off Norway. That was a bad day.

At home, Stephanie insisted on doing the shopping after lessons. Stephen and Steve and she ate a lot of stewed rhubarb out of the garden, sweetened by her with golden syrup on rationing points, because the sugar made from sugar beet had practically no taste. She did what she could with whale meat, but it would have taken Escoffier to drown the fishy taste. She studied Lord Woolton's advertised recipes featuring Potato Pete, potatoes being about the only thing available off ration apart from parsnips, swedes, and turnips, which the three of them united in hating, and carrots. The carrots she censored because their only merit was that they were said to improve R.A.F. eyesight. She wanted to go to sea. The household's favorite dinner was her invention of raw potatoes patiently grated, mixed with dried-egg powder and water, and fried as fritters in whale oil with a slice of the prized but rationed Spam. There was plenty of rabbit. Stephen, a very tall, thin man, would help himself to a piece of bread and margarine after he thought she had gone to bed. She never failed to hear the rattle of the bread bin. He found himself growing in love with her, and remarried when she was fourteen. Stephanie withdrew. Her stepmother was crass. Stephanie was not so much sad as amazed. Being in the habit of making lists in her five-year diary, she entered, "Difference between distress and dismay."

AFTER the war, big houses were so impossible to run that they were going for a song. Stephen bought back the old house for his growingly enormous new family from the living he earned at the shipyard, where the other directors, who had held on to their shares in the company, had reduced him to the level of an employee. Stephanie went South. She earned a living at a paper-pattern shop, took her Ph.D.—Steve had been a fine teacher—and used the Westminster library every evening. Jobs progressed. She was a blithe conversationalist and funny.

At a garden dinner party in Notting Hill Gate, she was seated next to a famous philosopher with a face that made her eager to understand. The lower part of the face was cold, and it chattered with talk, but the eyes were warm, and the forehead was wrinkled through being lifted by incessant interest. But how the bottom half did harangue. He seemed to find Stephanie engrossing. Eating nothing and allowing her to eat nothing, he set her a mathematical problem about the weighing of twelve balls in a balanced scale to find out the single one that was heavier. Or lighter. The heaviness or lightness not being the point, only the difference. The answer had to be achieved in two weighings, or was it three?

"I'm sure a monkey could do it," said Stephanie. "I don't seem to be able to. You do it."

The philosopher looked delighted. Later, he took her up to dine in Hall at his old Oxford college.

"This is delicious Burgundy," she said, when she thought it all right for a woman to speak.

"Claret."

"What kind?"

"Can't you tell? We take the labels off here, of course, because everyone can tell and anyway it's decanted."

There were many long gaps in talk. A celebrated historian said something about poodles' making very good gun dogs. A French woman professor with a plait round her head and a face like a muffin was pointed out as being the expert who bought the wines for the college. "What a breakthrough for the suffragettes," said Stephanie, in the gay voice that she knew would cause no one to pay attention. The women were allowed to stay for the port. She had been warned in advance that the penance for that privilege was silence. Quiet as a Trappist, she was surprised to hear that these men over their port—confident, upholstered men—exchanged not political opinions or blue jokes but information about home carpentry by mail order. There was a place in Weybridge, apparently, where you could get nuts and bolts and screws by the pound for a third of the usual price. It seemed that each of the dons was engaged in making a bedstead or a library stool as a present for his wife, and one, a chattering historian, even a very tall desk for himself to write at standing up. "Like Hemingway, you know. Spain littered with these desks. Carpenters very good there. Desks probably better than the prose."

No longer surprised that women had never battled particularly for the right to stay for the port, Stephanie thought of many things. Of her father, of sailing, of photographs of her mother, of how much she wished she had had a brother or sister. Going back to the philosopher's rooms, she slipped because a strap on her sandal had broken. With the knowledge that he had of woodwork, he could have been the best to help.

"Well, go on, help," she said.

"How?"

"A hammer and some nails? Glue?"

"They're in our country place." (Our. She hadn't known that he was married. Never a mention.)

"Or carry me."

He looked round the courtyard in case of onlookers. "Take both the sandals off and throw them both away later. They're beyond redemption."

"They're Yves Saint Laurent, and you don't throw Yves Saint Laurent away. I saved up for them. Thank you for dinner." She took the sandals off, carrying them as obviously as possible, and went to the station in bare feet. This was not her world, not her world at all.

After six months more in London, teaching Greek at the Polytechnic, she went back North to live in the same old West Lodge. Her piano was still there. In the big house, Stephen had taken to reading more and more and working less and less. He seemed poorly but denied it. The house was beginning to sag with books. His second wife, Sandra, must certainly have had her saving graces, but Stephanie found them hard to detect. Sandra read expensive Harrods books on roses and new ways with basements. Her children, now five of them, were brought to her regularly at five o'clock for tea by Mrs. Watson, who was revived beyond words by the sight of Stephanie. And Steve was still there, tutoring the new batch.

Living uncertainly in the lodge, playing the piano and thinking about jobs, Stephanie one night found a note slipped under her door. "HURRAH! BRAVO! WELCOME!" It read like a telegram from far away, but when she quickly opened the door Steve was outside in the rain holding some papers and a collapsible music stand under his mackintosh. They tried to shake hands, for some reason.

"I suppose we could go in," she said.

"You're already in." She thought briefly of carrying him over the threshold, remembering the philosopher's signal failure about her sandals. She was wearing them now, mended with glue, by herself.

"Is there something wrong with your leg?" said Steve.

"I have to be careful about the glue in my sandal. The

directions said 'Set under a heavy weight for twenty-four hours.' You can't exactly pile *The Decline and Fall* onto a sandal, so I thought it would work if I stood on it."

"Don't tell me you stood up for twenty-four hours for the sake of a sandal."

"No, I did it in shifts. Eight hours, three days. What are you carrying?"

"Some music."

"Whose?"

"Mine."

"By who?"

"By me, I meant. I've been composing a bit."

His pile of music paper was twelve inches high at least, and the music stand, which had a lip no higher than an inch, was at an angle of forty-five degrees. He played for her, leaping up now and then to alter something in his manuscript, and each time he did it the papers naturally scattered. When it was five in the morning and the papers had been collected by the two of them for the fortieth time, she said, "Would you mind if I meddled with the screws on the music stand?" He said nothing, troubled about getting the papers straight, and she did what she had been wanting to do for hours, which was the obvious matter of turning the screws with a penny so that at least the stand was level.

"Oh dear, I know I had a useful diminished seventh somewhere," Steve said from the floor, defeated by the muddle of his manuscript pages. His notation was small and beautiful.

"What key?"

"Submediant in the bass, in C minor, I think."

She played it.

"Yes. Or try it in the relative." Which she did. "That's better. Let's write that down somewhere where we won't lose it."

"The best place would be the place where you want it, wouldn't it?"

Another twenty minutes and the notes were in the manuscript. Steve lay down on the sofa. She played the passage for him to make sure it was what he wanted, not noticing that he had gone to sleep. The music was rapid and exuberant and quite new to her ear.

"I'm sorry, I dropped off. I know the music too well, you see," he said when she stopped. "Are you tired?"

"Play Scott Joplin," she said. She danced a bit. Then he made a cassette of himself playing Scott Joplin, and they danced together.

They had breakfast. No time to go to bed. He had to leave his bacon and tomatoes half eaten because he was due up at the big house to teach the children.

"What subject?"

"Latin for the older two. The little ones are doing what I think they think I think is finger painting. It looks a lovely mess to me, much like your being allowed to lick the bowl of raw cake mixture when I was teaching you. But you can make a packet now with finger painting, at the right gallery. One boy of three should have done marvelously out of it. By rights."

"What happened?"

"They swiped what he'd earned, his parents, and put it in trust for his children."

"Trusts, overbearing wills. It never works. Look at Daddy. Is he O.K., do you think?"

"He misses your mother." To avoid betrayal of Stephen's new wife, he got quickly onto his bicycle to whip himself along the drive. Stephanie was pleased to see that he didn't any longer use bicycle clips. When he had first come into the family, the bicycle clips had seemed immutable. He had often worn them when he was teaching her. It struck her how untrue the psychiatrists' truism is that people don't change. Her father, she had heard, had been a hypocrite and self-absorbed in the days before she was born, but look at his history since. And look at the disappearance of Steve's bicycle clips. To her, bicycle clips had perfectly exemplified caution. But now there was humor and boldness, which led to their spending the next night together. In the interval of that day she had got a job as a classics teacher in a faraway village, Cumberland not being all sheep.

IN the big house, Stephen said to Stephanie, "Having an affair with Steve?" She didn't answer, thinking the answer obvious, and Stephen said, "This is your father, Stephen, speaking, Stephanie. Steve?" Outside, the nanny was shouting, adding to confusion, "Steph and Stephie, come here at once if not sooner." The child—which child, all of them similarly encumbered by the now emptied but still onerous ancestral will?—came running and said in strong protest, "I couldn't be here sooner than sooner." The overheard incident reminded Stephen of his first wife, and he smiled at Stephanie, who was laughing.

"Look on it as euphony," he said.

"Darling Daddy, the names in this house are so impossible now that it would be better even to be called Euphony than Stephanie."

He tried the word for sound, didn't care for it, and said, "Clearly, you are Stephanie, because your mother was, and you are very like her."

"And you are Stephen. I don't forget that you called the ship H.M.S. *Talbot*. The ship you built in the Depression. Have you got any photographs of her before she was sunk? I don't know about her history. The records aren't very good. I looked things up in the newspaper library and the Admiralty."

Stephen pulled some dog-eared photographs out of his old navy-blue wallet, which was full of holes. Stephanie noticed its age and kind, and determined to find a new one exactly the same. He sorted the photographs carefully. She could see that there were many of a woman, and many others of a baby, but he kept these on his lap. His hands were arthritic but strong, and he had the sort of eyes often seen in the stock of the North of England, so brown that they are nearly black. He had never had need of spectacles. He handed over the photographs of the *Talbot*, christened after her, of course, as she well knew. There were pictures of every stage of the ship's building; even a photograph of the victuallers, North-country faces, thin, with bony features and big eyes. Engineers, fitters, a woman she didn't recognize. "That was Mary," he said. "The secretary who stayed on. All stayers, that lot. I can see you've got to the launching. Down she went, down the slipway, everything perfect. There wasn't any champagne, of course. We used cider. We couldn't do anything for her when she was torpedoed. Thirty-two of the men were saved. You won't remember, but you came out in one of the search boats with me." He paused, said, "It seemed the right thing to do, considering the bombing and all the rest of it. You were likely to be killed anyway. That's all past but not over, don't you know. I don't think my heart would go out to anyone who didn't love ships."

She played a Handel saraband for him on the harpsichord he had refused to sell. He listened without moving and approved, saying nothing. "And there's Steve, and he tells me you've learned Greek, and I want to take you to the shipyard, and there's grouse for dinner. You'll come, both of you. That would be my hope."

# Teeth

"WHY don't you get married, darling?" said Mrs. Chancellor to her daughter, Amanda. "Are you living with that dentist?"

Mr. Chancellor was on a bay horse, forging through branches along a green tunnel of path in Windsor Great Park. She was in front. Amanda was on a black mare. She is a sculptor. Pretty. Taut young figure. There was the sound of twigs crackling and leaves being swept aside. The riders ducked.

"I said why don't you get married? I asked if you were living with that dentist. Sorry. Did that branch hit you?"

Amanda said, "Didn't hurt. Living with, er, that dentist. Yes, I am. Well, no." She ducked another branch. "I'm not actually *living* with him. We're in different houses. He says we're living together, but I keep saying living together means *living* together. Having both of us and his razor all in the same place at the same time."

"But he's a dentist, Amanda."

"Yes. So?"

"If only he were a doctor, or even a vet."

"He's a very good dentist."

They came to a copse and made a halt in the ride. Horses tethered, Mrs. Chancellor passed Amanda a thermos flask of steaming coffee."I suppose it means he understands your oxyacetylene welding, though."

"What?"

"His being a dentist."

"Filling a hole in a wisdom tooth hasn't got much to do with sculpture," said Amanda.

"But something."

"More than you and Daddy have in common, you mean?"

Mrs. Chancellor accepted that tacitly. Pause. "We're fine," said Mrs. Chancellor. Pause. "It doesn't matter." Pause. "Politics draws us together. We got engaged at a very political time. He never minded my being a Tory. I wish your vet were a Tory."

"Not vet. *Dentist*. Could you call him 'him' or 'Andrew'? You did when you met him."

Mrs. Chancellor struggled with plastic glasses full of coffee and tried to make a level place for them in the grass to prevent them from burning her fingers. "Your father always managed to be a Socialist even when I did well on the Stock Exchange. He never took a penny."

"What's the matter with the glasses?" said Amanda. "Are they burning you?"

"Plastic carries the heat."

Amanda drew two silver cups in leather holders from a saddlebag and gave them to her mother.

"When do you and Andrew use these? I pictured you with enamel mugs. Something more earthy," said Mrs. Chancellor.

"They're for you. They're a present."

Mrs. Chancellor inspected them, taking the cups out of the leather holders and looking at the hallmark. "George III."

"I was waiting for the right moment."

"Did you make them?"

"No, I'm afraid not. I'm working in steel at the minute, and I knew you wouldn't like steel cups. You'd have called them mugs."

"You think I don't like your work?"

"Yes."

"The women in this family have always done things, darling."

"Your playing the Stock Exchange?"

"Despite Daddy. But we gave the winnings to Uncle Willie. I do it instead of bridge. I used to like bridge, but you never took to it and I can't abide having to collect a four."

Amanda said frantically, "Why doesn't Daddy like your betting on the Stock Exchange? Don't you want him to keep you company?"

"Perhaps it's that in the case of *doing* things one does them best alone. Like welding, I daresay. But I wish you'd marry Andrew."

"Even if he isn't a Conservative?"

"That could be changed, darling. One doesn't *live* best alone."

ANDREW's surgery is visible from the Fulham Road. There are reflections of chimneys in his windows. He was drilling a middle-aged male patient's tooth. The sound of the drill was mixed with John Cage music. The record came to an end. Andrew stopped the drill but left a hooked steel thing bubbling in the patient's mouth as he turned the record over on the gramophone beside his instruments. His stereo equipment is beautiful. Andrew is a tall, thin young man with horn-rimmed spectacles. He was wearing blue jeans under his dentist's white coat. Thick curly hair; thin nose; a decisive, modest temperament. He once agreed strongly in a dream with an imagined man who looked all too like himself; the man confessed to fear that he lived on the opinions of others. But in Andrew's waking life he has much resolve.

Above the record, Andrew said, trying to help his patient give his mind to the music instead of to dentistry, "Isn't that interesting?" Silence. "Or would you rather have the Beethoven late quartets?"

The patient said, through the instrument in his mouth, "No. I haven't heard John Cage before. One doesn't often get the chance."

"This is a new issue. These are also new speakers. Though I'm afraid you're not hearing the music at its best, with my working on you. I had the speakers specially positioned for the patient's chair." He waited again to go on working, drill poised. "All right? What a musician! I know it seems a pity to hear him through the bubbling. If you should be in acute pain later, feel free to take an aspirin."

The patient said, "Just a minute, could you? My mouth aches when I laugh." There was the sound of a door key being used, and footsteps. "Or are you in a hurry? Is that your wife?"

"No. It's Amanda. You've met her." Andrew carried on drilling, gently. "All right? Only two minutes more. It could be *two* aspirin. Shall I stop?"

The patient said, "Sorry. Aspirin as a pain cure always strikes me as funny." Andrew put on another John Cage record; the patient took the bubbling instrument and the wadding out of his mouth. "Excuse me, old friend, I'm not talking as a patient, but why don't you get married to Miss Chancellor? I was very struck by her when you introduced us."

Andrew thought, the drill in his hand. "It might wreck her career, you see. A sculptor is not cut out for marriage." And then, to defy his dream, "I don't live on the opinions of others."

The patient voluntarily put the instrument and the wadding back into his mouth and guided Andrew's hand to the tooth in question, nodding. He said, mumbling through the John Cage record and the bubbling, "I can see you're one of those chaps who worry about other people's problems. It's just a tooth to me, and it shouldn't be a grief to you."

IN Andrew's black-and-white kitchen, there is a small water heater over the sink. Black-and-white tablecloth with black-and-white napkins. In the big space—for sleeping, eating, talking— that extends from the kitchen, a spread of cushions around a white V-shaped sofa. A slate floor, a low round white marble table with objects on it, lit by a black hanging lamp with points of white light coming through punctured holes. White muslin curtains blowing in the breeze.

Amanda was wearing white jeans and a white silk shirt, with her hair pinned back in a ponytail. She had turned up her sleeves to cook, but she had stopped for the moment to go through a first-aid box, with Andrew's pair of spectacles lying broken beside her. Andrew had changed from his dentist's white coat into a navy polo-necked cashmere sweater and brown velvet trousers. Over this, though, he was putting on yet another white dentist's coat.

Amanda said, "You don't need a dentist's coat for dinner. It's going to get bouillabaisse all over it. It's already got a bit of my makeup on it."

"You may be right." He took the coat off. "I can't see much without my spectacles."

Amanda tried a gauze bandage on the broken bridge of the glasses. "They're too *loose*. They shouldn't have fallen off when you were just bending over a record. Supposing they'd fallen onto a patient."

Andrew said, "They're not loose generally. Only when I've had my hair cut. I had it done today."

"Would you mind an Elastoplast for the spectacles?" Amanda said. "There's nothing to be done about your hair. Have a look at the soup." She mended the spectacles, winding the Elastoplast round and round the nosepiece, watched by Andrew, who peered at the task and then at the bouillabaisse.

"When can I try the specs?"

"Have a go now."

Stopping the bouillabaisse-stare, Andrew put on the spectacles. Amanda started to wash mussels at great speed. Andrew looked cautiously into the pot, holding his spectacles with his forefinger. "What is it?"

"Don't you know? I said. Bouillabaisse. Mussels and things."

"Are all sculptors such good cooks as you?" He looked into the saucepan with apprehension. "Oh, I see. Mussels? I was afraid they were turnips."

"The mussels are the ones in the shells. Those are potatoes."

"When did you do all this?"

"This morning, early, before I had to pick something up at the foundry. I thought it would be all right to have garlic as it's Friday, but then I realized you might have a patient on Saturday and wouldn't want it, so I may make do with onions and dill."

"Yes, I could try that. Dentists can't be garlicky." He touched her neck. "Thoughtful of you. I have got a patient."

Amanda laid the table.

"What is it?" said Andrew.

"You see, that's where it would help if we were living together. Then I would know if you had a patient."

"That pot's too heavy for you. I'm stronger." He grinned, holding on to the Elastoplast. "My vision's now eighty percent better."

"Only eighty percent. Oh dear."

Andrew shut each eye in turn. "Or rather, I should have said a hundred percent in each eye separately but only eighty percent together. I think the glasses are not quite aligned, maybe. I don't like wasting your time. I'll get them done on Monday."

"I could do a more decent job on them in the workshop."

She had been holding a heavy black iron pot as she talked, absorbed by his spectacles problem. She put the pot on the table and looked at his hands. "Dentists always have nice hands. Mine seem to be full of clay dust and the nails are broken, however much care I take." Andrew took hold of one of her hands and kissed it.

After the bouillabaisse and starting to wash up, Amanda piled the plates in the sink. Andrew laughed and moved her over, using soap powder and a washing-up bowl.

"*Why* will you not let me wash up?" said Amanda.

"Darling, you're a terrific cook, but you're lousy at washing up. You go too fast."

"I've done those," said Amanda, watching him rewash some plates.

Andrew looked at her.

"With eighty percent vision they must look done, at least," she said.

"If I leave them on the sink rack, I'll think they're clean and put them away. Or the daily will."

"'What's the name for a daily who comes in twice a week?" Pause. "Andrew, do you want me to go?"

"Of course not. Hang on a minute. The iron saucepan can soak. Is it yours or mine?"

"Ours."

"I mean, shall I take it out to your van?" Andrew said.

"The van is full of bags of cement and thngs from the ironmonger. I found a beautiful piece of steel tubing that he gave me for nothing. And I had to get an oxygen cylinder filled up."

Andrew looked at her rubbing her foot. "What's the matter?"

"I've got a hole in my foot, I think."

"What?"

"I've dropped some molten steel onto it, and the steel seems to have made a hole in the bone." She studied the hole in her sock, then took the sock off. "It's a very small hole. Is it the sort of thing a dentist could fill?"

Andrew bent down to look at her foot and said, shaking his head about his ineptitude, "No, a doctor. Doctors are better."

"You sound like Mummy. Mummy's never going to get over your having spent your birthday-present money for me on a van."

"Sweetheart, you couldn't put bags of cement into the back of a Jaguar. I suppose that's what she wanted. But you're quite right that she doesn't think I'm up to standard. On account of the van. No more than she's ever going to get over my being a dentist."

"Or my working. Or our not living together."

Andrew pushed up his bandaged spectacles to finish the bouillabaisse pot with wire wool, using one eye only to get the fishy remnants in focus.

*   *   *

AMANDA in her back yard. Black jeans this time. She was draping a clay molding of a head in a wet cloth. There were armatures of horses and leaping men and women standing in the yard. Many sparks from her welding equipment. She finished what she was doing and went in the van to buy maps from the little local shop that sold everything. "One to Dover and then French ones from Calais onward," she said.

She looked through the maps carefully. "And a knapsack." She also looked most seriously at different brands of chocolate. "Which of these is the most sustaining?"

"Are you going mountaineering?" said the shopkeeper.

"No. I just like to keep my van stocked up, in case."

"A van's a useful resource."

"I once heard my grandfather say that about his rabbit hutch. He said he didn't like his family a lot and that he was terrified of his governess but that the rabbit hutch was a great consolation."

"How do you come to have a van, if I may ask?"

"Someone who understands me gave it to me."

A FEW days later, Amanda was again in her back yard, with goggles on, using the welder. Her mother was at the gate, shouting at her over the noise. Eventually Amanda noticed and pushed her goggles up. "I'm sorry," she said. "I didn't hear you."

"You should be out somewhere, darling. Oh dear, this van instead of the nice young two-seater you should have. *And* living alone." Pause.

"Is that why you came?" said Amanda.

"I thought I'd find you in now. I knew that you generally worked through lunch. Whereas it's the essence of marriage to have lunch together, I used to think. Or now of living together. Even that." Pause. "But then, to tell you the truth, Daddy used to be on the telephone all the time at lunch anyway, so the maids started to give him something on a tray in his study." Pause. "I wish you had more fun."

"Darling, I do. My bloke just doesn't want to seem to spend the day with me."

"That's what I meant. If he's in love with you, though? There's room for you both in either place, from what you say." She looked up at Amanda's little house. "This would be a splendid place for a dentist."

"I think it's room in his head that he's talking about. Space to move."

"Would you like a present of a course to brush up your Greek? You'd meet people. We won't need to tell your father. He would think you were unhappy."

Amanda said, sitting on a trestle table, "I'd rather sell a few more sculptures." She got up again, summoning resolution. "Do you mind if I work while we talk?"

"You'd enjoy it, you mean? Yes, I do see that."

The voices of small girls—maybe not so small, maybe eleven—floated over the fence. One said, "What perfume are you going to use tonight?" Another said, "I can't decide. What are you going to use?" The first girl said, "I thought the one called Perhaps."

Mrs. Chancellor said, "Darling, on second thoughts perhaps this would *not* be a suitable area for a dentist. And you *certainly* shouldn't be living here alone with children going about talking like that. Daddy would have a fit." Pause. "I'm having a fit."

"Mummy, they were just schoolgirls who'd probably been wandering around the chemist's."

"They sounded like what your grandmother would've called 'girls of the town' to me. I've seen a lot of it, as a magistrate. Oh dear, I've broken part of one of your wire casts."

Amanda looked at it. "How did you do it? It's very strong."

"Worry."

Amanda inspected the armature and threw it experimentally across the yard to test its stamina. Everything but the damaged wire remained intact.

"You can see, darling, it's much stronger than you thought," said Mrs. Chancellor.

"How on earth did you bust it, then?"

"I said, I was worried about you."

"So you broke a piece off my horse." Then Amanda melted. "You must have iron fingers. You should have been a sculptor."

The telephone rang inside the house. Amanda picked up the nearest receiver, in the kitchen. Her mother waved and left, having mended the iron base of the armature with a strip of Elastoplast ripped off her own finger. Inside the house Amanda said to Andrew, "No, nothing in particular's happened. I'm sorry. Mummy's just bust something. Darling, yes, I'm off. France, I think. I'll ring you up when I'm across the Channel: no, I'll do it from a hundred kilometers inland, wherever that gets me to. I'm not sure. I've got the van piled up. I probably won't get farther than Dover, as usual. You couldn't come with me, I suppose? No, yes, I know you need to be on your own, and there are the patients." Explanation to herself, it seemed. "You need a rest from me. Hello? Hello? Oh, damn."

She went into the yard again, looked for her mother, found the hapless piece of Elastoplast on her armature. Laughed, as much as was possible in the circumstances. Another day of Elastoplast.

After a while, having mended the damage, she went back into the kitchen to ring Andrew. He was out. She had to leave a message on his answering machine. Difficult to speak privately to a machine, but she tried. "Darling, I waited for the bleep, I was hoping you were in, I was wondering if your Elastoplast's holding but I expect you've got another pair of glasses by now. I'd better set off." A sound signaled the end of the recording. She said to herself. "Oh, blast," and redialed the number. While the machine talked in Andrew's recorded voice and she couldn't yet be heard, she muttered to the air, "Perhaps I should say I'm a patient with an abscess and an impacted wisdom tooth. Then I *know* you'd ring back." Bleep sound. She talked. "Andrew, I couldn't get the last bit in before the answering thing cut off, but I was saying I thought I'd better be off now and obviously I wanted you to know. Write to the *poste restante* at Nice. . . ." The machine shut off. Amanda spoke softly to herself. "I wonder where you are, whether you're just not answering, whether you know that I love you and that this is the trouble about not living together. Best not said, I suppose."

AMANDA was in the Nice *poste restante* reading a telegram from Andrew. "Come quickly." She fled to the telephone and asked in French for Andrew's English number, but the connecting operators responded negligently to the idea of the call's being urgent. She drove very fast along the roads of France, reading maps beside her as she went.

In England, she put two pence into the nearest coin box, got the operator, was told to put in sixteen pence. She reached Andrew. "Darling, I've only got enough change for one go. You might have to ring me back. I'm at Dover seven-three-five-one-oh-six. I don't know the code. I called you from—" Click. The usual telephone hiatus. Andrew rang back. She said, "I was saying I rang you from Nice, but you couldn't hear. They cut us off. What? Yes, I've got the van. You said you needed me. I'll drive as fast as I can." He suggested, in a voice so calm that it worried her, that they meet at the Bear Hotel. She went along with him. "Yes, that would be about halfway between us, I suppose. You'll have booked a room, or do you want me to?" They were cut off again.

She drove very fast through the South of England. The Bear Hotel. Perhaps all would be well. She tried once to make an emergency call to the hotel, emergency services being free, but she had to agree that this was not a question of "Fire, police, or ambulance" and had simply to drive on. She got to the hotel, still hoping that all would be well and that this was an assignation. Andrew's car was there. She got out and sat beside him. He had a week's growth of beard on him and could barely manage to get out of his car to hold her.

"I raced," said Amanda. "Did it seem ages? Why haven't you shaved?"

"I can't manage without you." He talked too fast. "Could we go for a walk?"

"Will they keep a room this late?"

"What room?"

It seemed best not to say that he wasn't attending.

They walked round and round the country green. "You won't leave me, will you?" said Andrew. "I told you I had a map in front of me and that this is exactly halfway, but you were late."

"I still don't understand why you haven't shaved."

"I haven't been seeing any patients, if that's what you mean."

"I thought you'd booked a room," said Amanda.

"We've got plenty of rooms of our own. Two *houses* full of them."

Amanda stroked his hair. "That's what I mean." He jerked away from her. She said, "Do you want to sit down? You either talk so fast that I can't understand you or you wait ten minutes before you open your mouth. Why didn't your secretary notice you're stalemated?"

"I wanted to marry you, but I realized it wouldn't work. I'd spoil your career. I'd spoil your life if we got married."

"Why?"

He jerked away again. "A drill's too like a welding machine." Pause.

"Could you rest?" she said.

"I'm selling you short." He kept on saying it.

"No, my dove."

A church bell in the village struck two in the morning. They walked about for a long time, going back to the hotel car park and driving to the green in his beautiful old Alvis, which was done up with straps like a steamer trunk. They lay down together on the green on the tarpaulin they had brought from the back of her van. She tried to get him to rest. When that didn't work, she tried to get him to talk to her, but then he would sit up and almost fight her off, like a swimmer in trouble grappling with a rescuer. In the way that banality has of interrupting crisis, a policeman with a torch suddenly loomed up and shone the torch at her.

"Having trouble, Miss?" the policeman said.

Amanda said, "Thank you. No. It's *my* tarpaulin." "Tarpaulin" was the first word that came into her head in the effort to make eloquent Andrew's straits to a stranger, and the absurdity was some mild relief.

The policeman persisted. "Your car, Miss? Your husband, is he?"

Andrew roused himself. "No, it's my car, and I'm not her husband, officer."

The policeman said, "So it's your car, is it, you say? Number of vehicle?"

Andrew looked for help to Amanda. "What's the number of the car, darling?"

"I don't think I've ever known," she said.

The policeman looked at the back of the car and wrote in his notebook, speaking out loud as he did it. "Can't remember number of own car, so-called. Lying on the grass with girl not his wife. Driving license? No driving license on him, witness asserts."

Andrew said, "It'd ruin her career if I married her."

Amanda looked at him gently.

The people at the police station were unexpectedly benevolent. They kept Amanda waiting outside a night cell but gave her news of him.

Next morning, while walking back to their parked cars, Amanda asked Andrew why he had kept saying all night, according to the police, that it was a bad time.

Andrew said, "Because I'm ruining your life. You just come and wash up."

"No I don't. You won't let me. You leave me the interesting part."

"What interesting part?"

Amanda: "Cooking."

"Cooking's a burden to a sculptor. I'm a burden to a sculptor."

"No." She remembered that a police inspector in the night had said, "He keeps putting those broken spectacles on in the cell. He says someone he's fond of gave them to him and they're not a very good mend and they give him double vision, and then he's able to go to sleep."

FAMILY conclave. Mr. Chancellor, Mrs. Chancellor, sitting in their drawing room. Amanda crouched on a footstool. Mr. Chancellor sitting at his desk, looking at a Reg Butler sculpture on it of a naked woman with her arms upstretched, shrouded as if in gauze by the dress she is taking off. Next to it, an Elisabeth Frink head of a warrior. A chintz-and-Chippendale room with a big log fire and many books. A Labrador on Mr. Chancellor's feet. He played often with the dog and, more often, pretended not to be hearing. Amanda's arcane ways alarmed him. A sculptor living with a dentist.

"Thank God you decided against him," said Mrs. Chancellor.

"I didn't," said Amanda.

Mrs. Chancellor said, "I didn't want to influence you, but a *dentist*. Henry, you know what you feel."

Mr. Chancellor said, "What? Of course I know what I feel. Oh, I see, you want me to say what *you* feel." He turned to Amanda. "Your mother feels that a dentist is not up to scratch for you."

Mrs. Chancellor said, "Your father's often said that if only Andrew had been a surgeon we wouldn't have minded."

Mr. Chancellor said, "Never said any such thing." He played with the Labrador with his foot.

"We don't even actually *live* together, technically. He could not see me anytime. Daddy, I think he's troubled. Whenever I go over to him now, he keeps picking fluff off his pajamas."

"He's in *bed?*" said Mrs. Chancellor.

"I put him there, but he won't stay there. He wants to get on with things. He hates holidays."

"So do you," said Mrs. Chancellor.

Mr. Chancellor said, "My experience is that people don't stand suffering well when they're in bed."

"He's stopped even being able to speak to me. It's as if he's got dentist's wadding in his mouth," said Amanda.

Mr. Chancellor said, "I think he means that he feels he shouldn't speak to you, perhaps. In case it causes you distress."

His wife said, "In any event, it's just as well."

Mr. Chancellor said to his wife, "Dear, it would be different if Amanda hadn't got such a lot of skeletons in the cupboard."

Amanda stood up and went to the desk to look at her father. Mrs. Chancellor said, "Skeletons?"

"Me, for instance," said Mr. Chancellor.

He plugged in an electric kettle and warmed a teapot from a tray, heating it over the fire. He wished to save the maid trouble.

"You?" said Amanda.

"That's the sort of thing he means," said Mrs. Chancellor. "A Socialist for a father. It's ridiculous for a busy man to be making tea just because the daily's lying down."

"She's not feeling well," said Mr. Chancellor.

"Good heavens," said his wife. "No one's well around here. The whole conversation seems to be about invalidism of one sort or another. People need to pull themselves together."

Amanda said, considering talking on behalf of her father but rejecting it, "Mummy, Andrew's going to be all right."

Her mother said, "The trouble with your father is he won't use his elbows. And Andrew's out altogether."

Amanda said, "It's my fault he's gone silent." Pause. Pondering her words: "He thinks he would get in my hair, you see."

Mr. Chancellor said, "Anyway, it was never anything much but pain for you. Was it?"

Amanda went over and helped him with the tea tray. "Darling, it was always one of the best things that ever happened to me," she said.

Mrs. Chancellor said, "Masochism." Mr. Chancellor looked at the Labrador and then at his daughter.

She said, "Of course, I may have bungled it hopelessly. Beyond recall, I mean."

Mrs. Chancellor said, "It's over anyway, quite rightly. I'd seen it coming." And then, to her husband, forcing him: "Hadn't we?"

Amanda said, "I haven't. I'm not giving up." She looked at her father, and he nodded.

"I wish I could help. Your mother seems to have it all organized," he said.

Mrs. Chancellor spoke over him to Amanda. "There's a nice, clever young man coming to drinks and I expect he'll want to take you out to dinner. You've got to promise to be good to him, because he was having an affair which has just broken up."

Amanda said, "Oh, darling, if you said that to me about him, what did you say to him about me? The same?" She looked at her father. "Daddy, the same?"

"Roughly," said Mr. Chancellor. Pause. "I'm afraid I've made things difficult for you most of your life. Weak of me, probably. I think you *might* like this man. Your mother does. His name's Jasper. I think he's probably a twit. But he's written several Fabian pamphlets."

"What about?" said his daughter.

"The last one was rather difficult to follow, for me, but it sold out. He seems to have a populist touch."

His daughter said, "What was it called?"

Mr. Chancellor said, "It was about Freud. I have always thought Freud a great prophet and possibly a left-winger. Your Conservative dentist isn't by any good luck a turncoat, is he?"

Amanda answered, "No, he isn't." Pause. "What's the pamphlet called?"

Mr. Chancellor said, trying not to cause further trouble by looking at her, "'The Libido Off the Leash,' I seem to remember."

AMANDA and Jasper walked, without finding much to say, in the garden of her parents' house. Mr. Chancellor could be seen in the window of his library, writing.

"Daddy's working," said Amanda.

Jasper said, in a rather high voice, "Your mother's the more interesting one, don't you agree? Though I noticed you talked mostly to your father. When we were having sherry, I mean," and anything he had meant melted into a high laugh.

Amanda said, "I'm sorry. Is it that you're sad about your girl?"

"All for the best. You sound well out of your chap."

"Ah. I'm glad you think so. Shall we go in? It's starting to rain."

Jasper put up the umbrella. "I always carry a brolly. I suppose I should take you out to dinner."

"It's only six o'clock still. No, six-fifteen. We can't possibly walk in the rain for two hours. Though I suppose we can't give up in front of Mummy and Daddy."

"No, that would be dropping a bit of a brick, wouldn't it?" Pause. Witless. "I tell you what, I've got a brilliant idea, I'll take you home. Are you a walker? I hope so. I'm rather a keen walker. I get jumpy legs at plays and reading books and things. Where do you live?"

"Miles. We could get a bus."

"Where to?"

"My dentist's, I think."

A look of distress on Jasper's face. But here at last something for him to do. "Poor girl, which tooth? Show me. Open your mouth."

"I feel like a horse having its age told."

"I've got a splendid, frightfully expensive dentist in Harley Street who would see you tomorrow morning if I rang him up. What's your name again, actually?"

\*   \*   \*

AMANDA and Jasper, he with his black City umbrella, walked for two hours. Little to say. Outside Andrew's house, they saw Andrew at work through the lighted window of his surgery. Jasper said, gallant, searching for a topic, "Aha! I spy a patient in the throes! Are you sure he's any good, practicing all the way out here? We could've run to a taxi. Does his receptionist work late?"

Amanda was already halfway up Andrew's steps, getting wet as Jasper tried to hold the umbrella over her. "He doesn't need a receptionist as late as this. I've got a key."

"A key to your dentist! I say, how grand. While you're waiting for your appointment, shall I come in and read you one of my pamphlets? Some of it's rather abstract."

"No, really not. The thing is, he doesn't seem able to talk at the moment."

"How peculiar." Jasper peered at Andrew through the window. "It isn't as if he's got any instruments in *his* mouth."

She kept silent. Nonspeaking, beloved Andrew.

"I'll give you a buzz," said Jasper. "What about getting sort of engaged? It could be unofficial, if you liked." He pursued her up the steps and put the umbrella over her in a way that touched her, in spite of the impossibility of their hours together. He gave her a copy of his pamphlet with his telephone number written on it. He kissed her. She saw Andrew catching sight of them but could hardly do anything except return the kiss and take the pamphlet. Then she shook Jasper's hand and watched his back disappearing in case he should turn round. He didn't. Disconsolate? It seemed not so, not at all. She sped into Andrew's house to tell him her shame about what she had said by mistake to Jasper on the doorstep. It released his tongue and soothed his concern for her. They talked far into the night, as they always had, as they always would. In her excitement about seeing Andrew, she had bade Jasper good-bye with the words "It was nice meeting me."

# When Are You Going Back?

"How is your sister these days?" said the owner of a chefs' outfitting shop in Soho. "You must miss her. She went back the best part of a year ago, as I recall. Are you the older or the younger?"

Juliet said, "I don't have a sister."

The owner said appreciatively, measuring her waist, "She's full of fun, isn't she? You're the spitting image of her. You must get a lot of people saying that. Though she's taller, isn't she. And so where do you both come from? I remember serving her a pair of trousers like the ones you're after now and I think she said Idaho. Or was it Ohio?"

"Cincinnati."

"Geography was never my fiercest point. I imagine she'd be the younger, wouldn't she?" He took her inside leg measurement and shook his head for some reason.

"No, you see, those were always my trousers and I want another pair exactly the same because I've dribbled paint on them from painting a tub."

"You're saying you're the same person. Well, I can verify that by the trousers now you've explained it. It would be the same blue and white checked trousers with the bagginess taken out."

"Do you always identify people by what they buy?"

Taking this to be a compliment, the owner of the chefs' outfitting shop bowed over Juliet's hand and said, "It's my profession, isn't it?"

"When will you have the trousers ready?"

"It's a big alteration but we'll be ready for you at the end of next week. Give my regards to your sister when you write to Cincinnati. I'll remember that now. It's in my head." He tapped his forehead. "Safest place to keep things."

A man waiting at the counter said, "But she hasn't got a sister, she said."

"Good morning, Mr. Neal," the owner responded, and then shouted down his back stairway and said, "Help up and in a hurry, we've got the butcher-boy trousers standing here inside-leg thirty-six."

Mr. Neal, a good-looking man of fifty-odd, said to Juliet as she was leaving the shop at speed, "Don't distress yourself. How long have you been here?"

"A year, in a dump, after a quick exit from Cincinnati to 'New York, New York, it's a beautiful town,'" which she sang.

"What do you do?"

"I'm at the London School of Economics on a grant. The new pants, trousers, are because of doing up the dump."

"I heard. And you like it here in spite of all, and you're about twenty-two?"

"Twenty-three and I'm called Juliet and thank you for catching on." She went quickly into Old Compton Street.

FRIDAY morning. By tube to a lecture at the London School of Economics. Juliet was wearing a spotted muslin dress under a thick coat that her parents had sent her from Cincinnati, thinking that anywhere so far across the Atlantic was likely to be freezing. The coat was far too hot for London, but the fragility of the muslin dress made up the difference. While they were waiting for the L.S.E. lecture to begin, Juliet told an English girl named Harriet about a dream she had had the night before.

"You threw an india-rubber at me," said Juliet. "An eraser."

"I'd never do a thing like that."

"Harriet, I know you wouldn't, but in the dream you did. You also flicked some ink at my dress and it spotted it."

"It's spotted muslin already. Where's the spot?"

"English people are so literal. It was a dream."

"But you wouldn't have a dream without a reason." Harriet searched Juliet's dress and said, "There's a faded spot here. You've no right to have a dream like that."

"It was followed by a crummy business in a caterers' clothing place."

"What happened?"

"A man kept on sending messages to my sister when it was me he was measuring and I haven't got a sister anyway."

"Was that another dream?"

"It happened, and it's always happening here. People are always saying 'Oh, are you here?' or 'When are you going back?' They don't mean to be rude but do I have to wear a label around my neck? I'm beginning to feel like an ecto-morph."

"Good heavens," said Harriet. "You've been here long enough, haven't you? You're not that much of a solipsist."

Talk bogged.

"Say something," said Juliet.

Harriet shook her head. "I've got nothing worth saying at the moment."

Juliet said, "You're turning me into someone garrulous and I'm sure I'm not."

"I'm not up in Freudianism." Harriet went on reading *Language, Truth and Logic.*

Juliet said, "The Lord protect us from high-bred English silences." Wait. "I mean, you let a conversation go off the rails and then there are casualties and people are getting killed because the carriages are on their sides by then and you don't have the slightest idea how to hoist them up again and the hell with it."

Before the afternoon lecture Juliet found on the reading-flap of her chair a bottle of black ink and a note from Harriet saying "This is to fill in the faded spot or dot. Use a pen, not a brush, or the ink will run. I'm sorry about the dream." In a million years Juliet would not have thought her likely to have so acted on an insight. The note was signed "Anyway. H."

ANYWAY. Friday evening. Back to the dump, which was in Soho. Juliet shared it with two English girls: a gym instructress called Victoria, and a personnel manager called Joanna. The evening took the usual course of any other Friday evening.

"Have some sherry," said Victoria to Juliet. "I'm flaked, aren't you?" She looked at her watch and said, "No, Jim's coming in a moment to pick me up and they hate people being late for dinner."

"Who's they?"

"The people we're staying with. Upcountry."

"Derbyshire as ever?"

"The telephone number's on the kitchen pad but there won't be any calls for me. They know I'm always away for a Friday-to-Monday."

"It sounds forbidding. You always say a Friday-to-Monday but it's only a weekend, isn't it? You work yourself to a standstill on Friday and Monday so it isn't as if you had four days off."

"It's just what we call it," said Victoria. "It's not meant to seem foreign to you." She put her hand on Juliet's arm with a gentleness that Juliet associated with vets, Cincinnati, animals, a hen-house being built by her brother-in-law. "You must come up to us one day," said Victoria. "Let us know when you're free. It's not at all intimidating. It's a frightfully big house so you'd have all the room in the world and there aren't any rules apart from listening for the meal-gongs. It's not that sort of place. You're left alone as much as you want."

"I bet," Juliet said that, and then "Erase. Sorry."

"You really must come up one day. You'd enjoy it. I don't like the thought of your being here alone every Friday-to-Monday. Think about it and I'll put it to our hosts."

There was a honking car outside, and Victoria ran downstairs with her usual leather grip, after leaning out of the window to shout to Jim, "We have got saddle soap up there, haven't we?" Jim shouted up, "Do you want to polish the old grip?"

And there was Joanna still to go.

Juliet said, at the door of Joanna's room, "Is there anything you want? I'm going to do some shopping."

Joanna came out, looking vivid, with a bundle under her arm that she regularly pretended to be a load of food though both Victoria and Juliet knew that it was her clothes and books for the weekend at her boyfriend's studio. The silence about his name and her whereabouts had been shyly insisted upon for so long that even her flat-sharers observed the code.

Kicking the code, Juliet said, "To be practical, so what's his name?"

"Henry," said Joanna. "I'm just taking him some salami."

"Soho being rampant with salami, alive and kicking with Chinese bean sprouts, and would you both like to come and have dinner here with me tomorrow night?"

"I'd have to ring you. He may have fixed something."

"You don't have to fix salami. There's nothing to be done about salami. You just have it."

"One can put it in a cassoulet. When *I* said fixed something I meant he may have arranged something. He often does. For Saturday night. He's a bit difficult about weekends. Could you and I have pizza together on Monday night? I know Victoria's got people coming and we'd be in the way."

"You're sure you're free?"

"I've never heard you use sarcasm."

"It was an attempt to be funny."

"Yes." Joanna took her bundle from under the smock she was wearing and smelt it.

"Garlic. Henry doesn't like garlic much because of his ulcer."

"Salami *is* garlic. *Denotes* garlic. Anyway that's all clothes and books and notebooks."

Joanna looked bruised and said, "Honestly, there is some salami in here, though not all. I admit that, and I've found a place that does it with much less garlic than anywhere else so all one can do is hope. We'll see each other on Monday at seven and go out at once because it's not right this business of lurking when one of us is using the kitchen."

"I don't understand why we don't get asked."

"I know, but Victoria wouldn't see it that way. This way you've got the place to yourself all weekend."

"And I've got the paint-stripper for the tub so I've that to do."

On Saturday Juliet spent four hours in the empty bath patiently stripping yellowed paint off the original porcelain. The smell of the paint-stripper was noxious.

Harriet rang and asked her to a cocktail party that evening.

"I'm in an old pair of chef's pants because I'm stripping the bath and can't make it but thank you a lot," she said.

"How are you doing it? The bath."

"By sitting in it."

"Why aren't your flat-sharers doing it with you?"

"They're away for the weekend."

"Do you want me to come over?"

"Two of us in a tub already guaranteed to burn your skin off?"

"You shouldn't be left alone in a bath."

ANYWAY. Tomorrow was a Sunday. Of course, Juliet woke unusually early on this day to be rid of. She made coffee. Her Soho street was full of shops selling coffee beans out of huge sacks: beans that you were encouraged to run your hands through and to smell before you bought. She did some necessary work, found it engrossing for five hours, and then got out her address book and rang everyone she knew, including Harriet. No one was in. "One's forefinger gets fatigued with dialing. Also one's mind," she said to herself. It was a day and evening nearly impossible to get through, though reading Jane Austen helped. That grace of moral order.

EARLY ON MONDAY morning, she telephoned Harriet to ask her if she would choose some people to come to dinner far ahead in the Soho flat, and if she would do it now, before they were likely to have gone to work. Harriet did some quick telephoning and rang back. Dinner the Thursday after next. Married couples, all of them. "People do seem to get booked up. These particular people are more interesting than nice, if you know what I mean. I could have a look for an extra man for you at the L.S.E.," said Harriet; but Juliet said, "I'd be getting up and down with cooking and plates, and anyway who cares about *placement* now?" The phrase "extra man" rang in her head.

She cooked cassoulet, new to the peculiar ingredients ("pig's knuckle, or trotter if unavailable, a quarter of a goose . . ."). The butcher knew what she wanted. The one she liked best had a particularly beautiful shop window, with crowns of delicate lamb cutlets dressed in chef's frilled caps of miniature size. The cuts of meat were arranged on bright green artificial grass. She had never seen grass like this except in Hollywood. She thought of Beverly Hills, and the huge rolls of such stuff that were used for celebrities' dinner parties to protect the real grass.

She also made taramasalata. Her cohabitants in the flat helped with setting the table. They had asked their own boyfriends. Henry in person at last. Victoria's had brought his guitar. Juliet said to him, "Would you mind a lot if you played the piano instead? There's one in the bedroom. Or maybe you don't play the piano."

"It would mean cutting my nails. I need my nails for my

guitar." The nails were as long as a mandarin's.

"Yes, you'd regret it," said Juliet.

"Juliet's against regret," said Victoria, a ready translator of the clear.

"There's bound to be somebody else who can play a piano," said Juliet. "I suppose I even could, in spite of the cassoulet. It's only that we've had such a heap of guitar music at home since protest songs, and people sit on the floor in jeans, and there isn't much room for sitting on the floor here with three sofas in the room. Also, no one listening to guitar songs knows when they're going to stop. Whereas with a piano you do."

Some of the people who came, at helpful Harriet's suggestion, were politicians; some literary editors; some photographers; one a titled writer of an expensive and inept cookery book illustrated with witty drawings of disaster in the kitchen with *noblesse oblige* going on in the drawing room. A man who had been identified only as "Could-we-bring-somebody" was introduced namelessly as "This-is-who-we-meant." He was the Mr. Neal of the chefs' trousers encounter. Both he and Juliet remembered very well indeed. He came with her into the kitchen, which was as small as a broom cupboard.

"Something in the oven smells splendid. What is it?"

"Cassoulet. What are you called before Neal?"

"Nick. It's nice of you to have me. What can I do?"

"Remember for me where people are sitting. I've written it out on my hand." She showed him the palm of her hand with a table plan and initials on it in ink.

He studied the palm as if he were telling her fortune. Realizing what he must look as if he were doing, he said, nodding to the drawing-room-cum-dining-room, "Most of the people here aren't exactly lifelines." He soaped off the ink after he had convinced her that the two of them had safely committed the drawing to memory. She had put him on her right, but he said that the shadow minister present had to be on her right. So Nick, that source of help, was to be far away.

\*    \*    \*

"I ALWAYS wonder how long one has to soak real haricots," said an antique dealer named Clara in a tenth-hand Victorian evening dress that, as she explained loudly to no one in particular, had cost her a year's salary. Leaving no space for an answer, she said. "If it hadn't been for Christopher, who's getting thinner and thinner on his yogurt. . . . Sorry. Lost my way. Oh yes, if it hadn't been for Christopher living near his flea market I'd never have found it. Christopher has pull in lace."

"Twenty-four hours," said Juliet to Clara.

"What?" said Clara.

"The beans."

"Must have been awake all night," said a highly mooted Tory M.P. called Bertie.

"They don't need watching," said Juliet. But Bertie had the habit of making statements rather than asking questions, and he had already gone on to ask the table at large if anyone knew whether Piggy was still footing it in Nuristan.

"No," said a literary editor called, it seemed, Chips, "but Bimbie's still out there."

The wives, called Emma (two), Pit-Pony, Becca, and Caroline (two), listened carefully to their husbands and spoke across everyone willy-nilly about a distinguished couple from South Africa who had been under house arrest for five years. At last, mention of people whom Juliet knew about. She tried to get a word in about their pamphlets and the wife's novels.

"One *must* read something she's done," said Clara. "One hears about her books all the time."

"They do loom," said Bertie.

The witty artist drew a witty drawing on the back of his bread-and-butter plate. The ink would come off the plate, but not the butter now on the tablecloth, Juliet thought. Then the mooted young politician spilt his glass of red wine.

"Salt," said Clara.

"No," said the politician. "That turns it black immediately.

One trick. Foolproof. Pour some very *good* claret on it at once, and then wait three seconds and put at least half a bottle of Sauterne on it. Chemical reaction. It's got to be frightfully good Sauterne. I've seen it work even on Aubusson carpets. I daresay it's because of the age of the claret and then the counterreaction of the sugar in the Sauterne."

Equipped only with Chianti, it seemed to Juliet that it was going to be cheaper to buy a new tablecloth. The incident anyway passed in an instant, and only Nick looked at the cloth and then firmly got up and put soap and water on the mess.

"One still misses old Fruity," Bertie said out of the blue.

FOR a moment even Harriet forgot his invariable freedom from context and looked for fruit for him in the kitchen. This in spite of the Brie and salad on the table. And then she remembered that a man called Fruity had been Bertie's best friend who had died two years ago of an undiagnosed illness in the midst of writing what had promised to be an innovative book.

Bertie, Fruity, Bimbie, Piggy, Pit-Pony. "It's all names," Juliet shouted suddenly and very fast, crying; "I mean, I know they're your friends, but I don't even seem to get time to ask you about them." She ran down the stairs and out into the street for a few moments. No one noticed except Nick. When she came back she had mustered herself and said, so low that people at last attended: "Look. I know I'm American, and I don't expect you to have heard of Eudora Welty or Peter Fonda even, but there must be something English we could all talk about. Or some*one*, if that's easier. Inigo Jones? Sickert?" No luck. "Britten?"

"Oh, you mean the E.E.C.," said the mooted politician. "One doesn't think of it as Britain any longer."

"She means Benjamin Britten, I think," said Nick.

Pit-Pony leaned over for some Brie. Juliet asked her about her name. "It's because the family comes from rather near the mines, the coal mines, and I used to go to the cottages of the miners' wives who worked in the house because they let me do things more than the family, and often I'd stay with them overnight." She paused, and couldn't go on with the cheese. "It's very bad up there now. We don't know much down South. I wish people in London wouldn't call me Pit-Pony. Eliza's a perfectly good name up there. Do you feel a bit lost here, Juliet?"

Taking a cue of manners, as he saw it, the literary editor leaned forward to Juliet and said, "When are you going back?"

"She's here," said Nick. "Why do English people always ask that?"

"Why why?"

"Why what?"

"Why do you ask why?" said the literary editor.

"Bound to make anyone feel they've got no place here, isn't it?" said Nick. "Wouldn't it be more interesting to find out why she came?"

"Because of the L.S.E.," said Juliet, "and Shakespeare and Jane Austen and Harriet Martineau and the way English people love Nelson, and things." She looked quickly at Nick. "And other things."

"You haven't told us about the L.S.E. An exchange, was it?" said the shadow minister.

"No. I did it on my own." Ferocity, unusual in her. "And, apart from Shakespeare, I suppose Pope, Dryden, Swift, Chaucer, A. J. Ayer, Bertrand Russell, Purcell, the Beatles, as Harriet knows."

Nick stayed with her and helped with the washing up. Then he took her to his flat in Devonshire Street. For days they played truant and saw only each other, eating sardines or fried bread and tomatoes, walking in Regent's Park, looking at old bookshops, reading in bed.

"What exactly do you do?" she asked, after a couple of days spent mostly in the bedroom.

"Not much."

"But what exactly?"

"I was a waiter in Marylebone Lane, but I'll have got the sack by now for being absent without telephoning. I used to be a doctor but now I'm doing research. Being a waiter gives you time for thinking."

"That's what you mostly do?" she said, herself thinking, and then, "Could I be on the other side of the bed for a while?"

She climbed over him. He said, "Or I suppose it might be called thinking about thinking. I mostly keep a notebook and put things down that might lead somewhere one day. Also I'm learning electroencephalography. I'm teaching myself. I've got a place in a lab at hospital. Just being a G.P. didn't seem very adventurous at my age, so I chucked it at fifty."

"You talked about Hamlet in your sleep last night. I couldn't quite make it out."

"I put it down, whatever it was." His notebook was now on her side of the bed. "Look for it if you like. It's one but the last. It's only a note." She read, "Young man ransacking his mother for mislaid birthright of innocence. Magnanimous play." After that there was a note about electronics that she couldn't decipher.

JULIET dreamt of New York: of the noises of sirens, and car-horns, and transistor radios held to the ears of pedestrians; and of Central Park concerts where she had often stood in line since early in the morning with her bike and a picnic to hear some great singer in the evening from a place on the grass near enough to escape the hubbub of the streets alongside. She woke abruptly, waking Nick, and said, "I said 'waiting in line' in my sleep."

"I didn't hear it. Why does it matter?"

"It should be 'queueing.'"

"Only here. You were in New York in your head. Either's all right. It depends who you are."

"Not where you are?"

"Both people understand both sorts of English, unless they're duffers."

Nick went to work at the restaurant at eleven next morning, hoping that his job would re-offer itself. Juliet read all day, which was her way of going to ground, and forgot about lunch. The telephone rang. She had the common odd instinct, just before picking up the receiver, about who the call was from and that it was for her. So she said "Nicholas Jefferson residence here."

"And this is Nick's Diner speaking and would you like to come and have a rather nice dirt-cheap load of abroad dinner at six o'clock? The restaurant is Pakistani and we'll have to eat in the kitchen. The waiters wait on each other." He gave her the address. He gave her a map. He made her draw it for herself over the telephone. As though in readiness for a long foray, she put on espadrilles. Following the map, which she had again drawn on her hand just as she had the seating of people to dinner, she set off. Many doctors' plates in brightly polished brass. A soldiers' hospital named after Edward VII. In three minutes she had reached the restaurant. Nick being the man he was, he had not wanted her to wait and was waiting there himself at the door.

They had tandoori chicken. The chicken was hot, the kitchen very hot, the prices very cheap. Many of the people there, mostly men, were reading as they ate. Languages got mixed in her ears. The voices she had been reading: Flannery O'Connor, Burke, Beckett; and the voices she was hearing: Nick's, her own, Pakistanis', waiters' answering dinner orders in languages she couldn't understand or sometimes even place. Her own accent she found imprecise and slurred but Nick understood it well enough. Again, he saw where her attention lay, and he explained that a lot of young foreign doctors worked here when they weren't on call.

"Doctors in America earn a fortune."

"Not here. Not if they're working on their own time to be

specialists. Or if they're juniors on the N.H.S."

"I thought the N.H.S. was going downhill."

"Most people think that about everything about England, including a lot of English people and including some ex-left-wing waiters who've made a pile and taken to hunting. But some of them get it right. One who's got it dead right has been working so hard that he's just had a nervous break-down."

"Is he in a clinic?"

"No, he's working. He's got a job to do."

"Doesn't he need help?"

"What does that mean?"

"Psychotherapy?"

"Help doesn't mean that in England."

"Then what?"

He went through a few of his notions of help. Friends. Company. Books. Work, obviously. Humor. Sense of ances-try. He thought even of saying "Mercy," but put that aside and instead paid the bill, which turned out to be a matter of subtracting the amount from his wages. Juliet listened to the Tower of Babel sounds in the kitchen. He said, "This is what the big English cities are like now. Swinging London had always been a magazine invention. Gave rise to a great many very bad pizza places and a great many W.1. houses turned into gambling joints. W.1. is what abroad calls Mayfair. And estate agents, of course. There's a Czech playwright eating over there. He speaks English but he won't write in it. He says he can't. Terrible thing, for a writer to be plundered of his language. He signed the Civil Rights manifesto. That's why he limps. The police shot him as he was escaping but they only got his ankle. It's a very bad fracture."

Nick went into the dining room to work. She had the spare key to his flat. She did some unnoticeable housework for him, thinking to be useful. She had asked him again about whether she might read his notebook and, being an unfretful man, he had said, "Of course. They're not journals."

All the same, she waited until he came back, and then she read in another room after he had fallen asleep. One passage struck her because she had had no hint of the part of his mind that would have prompted it. A note about a man in the time of the Gospels, and his function in that society being accessory to his character, and society something he could control. "Now a man is an annex of his social function and there's nothing he can do when the bias of his character and the edicts of his job happen to conflict." And immediately after that, a note about her in the caterers' shop. About the clothes she wore, and then an exact report of the words, and then "Edicts of her undertaking v. instinct to quit?"

SHE thought about Nick: the way he had listened to things in Soho, the way he worked at the restaurant. She went to sleep in the room where she had been reading and dreamed all over again, word by word, the ungentle dinner party in Soho. Jumping awake from thirst after that was over, she had a drink of water and went immediately to sleep again until she was wakened by the noise of Nick shouting. She went fast into the bedroom and shook him awake. "You were having a nightmare."

"Was I talking in my sleep?"

"Screaming."

"No way to lead a platoon," he said, still in the nightmare. "Was it in the Ardennes?"

"I don't know."

"A tank's blowing up there. It's in flames. Six men inside. I can't see. My eyelids are too hot. Every time I run back to get one of the men out it gets worse."

"Sit up. You're still in the dream." She got him some hot broth because he kept saying, "Hot sweet tea."

"It's a *dream*." She thought of slapping his face, but it seemed quite the wrong thing to do. "It's not as though you're hysterical," she said, explaining out loud without noticing.

"One gave them hot sweet tea for shock," he said. "It was

all they wanted. There was one of them I couldn't get out."
At least he had moved into the past tense. He went suddenly
to sleep and she thought it best to stay this time. She
overslept, of course, to his scorn. He brought her breakfast in
bed. "You were talking in your sleep," he told her.

Not the moment to bring up the Ardennes, she said to
herself. Out loud, "What about?"

"New York. You do miss the sticks and stones of New
York, don't you?"

"Not in Devonshire Street. I thought eggs were short here.
You've given me a boiled egg."

"They're not short now. That was in the war. Forty years
ago. I'm very old for you."

"Old to be a *waiter*, perhaps, but not a waiter learning
electroencephalography."

"Old to be an extra man."

"Some phrase."

"Worse things. What exactly were you dreaming about?"

"That awful party."

"England isn't all like that. You won't skedaddle, will you?
I thought I'd go into the lab today. I think I may have left the
sterilizer on."

She bought food on the way back from the L.S.E., and a
kaftan, and started barbecuing steak on the toasting grill of
his gas cooker as soon as she heard his key in the door. The
place immediately reeked. She opened the windows and went
back to the stove. He yelled at her, turned off the stove, and
shouted. "Turn back those ridiculous sleeves, you idiot. You
can't do a cookout in a kimono. You might have been a
cinder."

"It's not a cookout, it's a cookin. This isn't the first time
I've cooked steak. And there's ratatouille."

"Garlic makes me sick."

The steak cooled. They went to bed without dinner. She
kept the ratatouille in the fridge, hoping for improvements in
appetite. That night she had violent dreams about petrol

thrown on to flames: because of the row, the flaming steak, the flaming tank. Next morning it seemed that he had had much the same dream. Things healed. They had the cold steak for lunch. "The ratatouille's still delicate ground," she said.

"Yup."

"Do you want to chuck it out?"

"Not on your life."

HE worked in a notebook and then among his long charts of electroencephalographs. She wrote letters to America. He said suddenly from the floor: "When I was on the tube yesterday a woman said her doctor had told her that her liver was on a knife-edge. That was how I felt about the ratatouille. But I shouldn't have shouted at you. I'm sorry."

"Well, you were in a war."

"I had a very easy war."

"I've heard a lot of Englishmen like you say that."

He thought and then gave a barking sort of laugh.

"What was that about?" said Juliet.

"My sister. She was the private secretary to somebody top-secret. She was the ideal private secretary because the most fascinating things went right over her head. She'd be reading women's magazines and serials and horoscopes, you see, between using her high speeds. So you can safely ask her about the most confidential decisions and she hasn't an idea what you're trying to find out. And so you could say that women's magazines won the war for us."

"At that dinner party, did you notice how people much too young to remember the war kept on saying how American food parcels kept Britain going?"

"There are pockets of English people who are condescending to America."

"But not your restaurant. There were a lot of very young American students there and they knew more about the Czechs than I do. They'd been there."

"I've been to America twice, actually. The Medical Research Council helped. Oh, by the way, I think I may have left the sterilizer on." She had begun to recognize this as a ploy. He said, "As it's a Saturday, we wouldn't be disturbing anyone if you came in with me. Would you like that?"

As if he were giving her a treat, he told her in the lab a little about electromyography. "It's a matter of sinking needles into the right place, basically." He laid himself down on the examination couch and told her to watch for what happened on something that looked much like a television screen. Green waves. She turned round, and shouted to him to stop, please.

"I thought you'd be interested. It doesn't hurt at all. I know what I'm doing." But he got off the examination couch. Juliet, feeling ashamed, took Nick to see a revival of a poor film called *Green Slime* because the title had always interested her. On the way out, he said, "We might go back to America for a while together, yes?" Having a careful mind, he added, "Before coming back, of course."

# As Is

"For you to be such a close friend of Professor Chalcott is a craziness," says Professor Anna Krzyżowska, a Polish émigrée physicist in a laboratory at an Eastern American university, to an English-born student named Fiona Cairns. It is 1969. "He's forty-five years older than you are. He'll die before you. Then where are you? Fiona, I ask you, where are you?"

"In the cupboard. Closet. Looking for a pipette."

"Did you hear what I said?"

"Yes. I'm in the closet. I think we may have lost that pipette. To be frank, I think you may have busted it."

"You're not answering my question."

"I told you, I'm in the pipette closet. The closet for pipettes."

"I think you would not recognize a pipette from a pipe," says Professor Krzyżowska, blowing into a complex of linked tubes and producing a sediment that gives her satisfaction. "What I said—and the correct response is not in my closet—was that it is a craziness for you to be such a friend of Professor Chalcott when he's forty-five years older than you are. And then I said he'll die before you. And then I said where will you be?"

"Without him."

77

\*    \*    \*

FIONA is nineteen years old. She is studying comparative literature, but to earn money for textbooks she helps in the physics laboratory. Cross about the pipette, Professor Krzyżowska says, "You're certainly not born to be a physicist."

"No. I know."

"And what is more, you are a foreigner," says Professor Krzyżowska unreasonably. "You even stumble over cupboards and closets. That is, over usage of cupboards and closets."

"I know."

"You failed to respond to my statement. I am so very tired of being treated as the Polish Corridor."

"I'm trying to forget which statement you mean."

"That for you to be such a close friend of Professor Chalcott must stop. You must protect yourself."

"Aren't those *injunctions?*" says Fiona, head in closet, crying.

PROFESSOR KRZYŻOWSKA, who pretends to a godmotherly role toward the pretty Fiona, feels herself to be ugly. It is beyond her confidence to see herself with the good wishes of others: to see the full mouth, the middle-aged nobility plucked out of danger. She has been forced to learn distrust, wishes to forget the learning, but finds it impossible to erase. The chalk marks of Poland's history are not to be washed off the blackboard of her mind. Sometimes when she tries to dream the phrase in English, "blackboard" becomes "backboard," and the next day her shoulders are braced and her neck is stiff as she lectures. Her courage is invisible to most and taken for severity. In the large and jealous frame that shelters her, she strenuously chides herself. She hides cost. Later that day, alone, she breaks an essential piece of her research construction. She, too, weeps. Then she works, speaking to herself in Polish. The true small self that aspires and chugs along in travail.

* * *

PROFESSOR CHALCOTT is of another stuff. He teaches musicology. His house is large and it sags with books. He was born there, married there, saw his wife die there, continues alone to entertain friends there with undiminished heed. "I'm eager to know what you have been reading," he will say. Innovation of any sort, in any field, excites him. "You've taught me something I didn't know," he will say, leaning his chin on his silver-headed cane, his dog at his feet. The dog is brown, and the Professor, typically, having spent some time pondering the question of a name for him, called him Brown. Fiona and he love and comprehend each other. He preserves that careful literalness, that adherence to presented facts, which is so often the staple of conversation in people brought up in houses such as his.

The day after Professor Krzyzowska's effort to detach Fiona from him, he comes into the university library. Fiona has just finished three hours of work as a junior librarian to earn another two dollars an hour. All the returned books are back on the shelves. As a last act of tidiness, she has been trying to clear a fellow-student in a yoga trance off a reading table.

"What are you doing?" Professor Chalcott asks her.

"I can't wake this girl."

Professor Chalcott peers at the cross-legged yoga practitioner, says nothing, and goes into the librarian's office. He drops down like a sack of flour into a green plastic armchair.

"Are you bored?" he yells. "I've been bored for the last ten minutes."

She lugs herself to the door and considers. "Yes, I am. But what would the option be?"

"Would you like to come to a magic shop? I'm bored with deciphering Beethoven's shorthand. I like you better than his quartet, now that it's ten past four."

THEY set off. Professor Chalcott wraps himself in a muffler and takes a bookbag and a briefcase. He says, "Can you decide on any way of avoiding the man at the reception desk? It's unpleasant of me but I don't care for him. A weakling and a dullard, I think. He has the sort of face that seems to want to swallow its chin."

So they climb a stairway, Fiona pausing in the pretense of doing up a sandal, to give Professor Chalcott a chance to catch his breath, and they leave by a door from another floor.

At the magic shop, Professor Chalcott is known not as a learned musicologist but as an expert in magic. He is warmly greeted. Shown things.

Professor Chalcott: "No, no, no, you know perfectly well I've seen the disappearing egg over and over again. Perhaps something with cards." He practices a trick needing both legerdemain and fast patter, and then says, "Arthritis puts the kibosh on that idea. Some silk scarves to vanish up the sleeve, in pretty colors? Colors that would suit my friend? Yellow, deep pink?" Again he practices with what the admiring manager produces. "Yes, that's within the range of possibilities. My physical possibilities, apart from possibilities of enchantment."

Fiona says to him outside the magic shop, "Professor Krzyzowska says we shouldn't spend so much time with each other."

"Because I'm going to die first, I suppose."

"I don't give a damn."

"Don't you believe her, anyway. I'm here. Beckett once said, 'The young pop off. The old hang on.'"

A SPARROW that appears to be blind in one eye then crashes into Professor Chalcott's briefcase. He picks the creature up and strokes it and then puts it into the briefcase, making a nest of his handkerchief for the bird and leaving the case open. "Do you know," he says to Fiona, "there are one thousand three hundred and fifty-nine feathers on a sparrow's neck? I fear this one may have lost a few."

"What a lot you know. Beethoven's shorthand, magic, sparrows."

"And you your languages, and being able to do a back-bend. Combined"—gaily—"we could take everyone on. I forget if it was Archimedes who said, 'Give me a lever long enough and I could lift the earth.' We'll look it up."

"I like it when you say that," says Fiona.

"What are you reading today?"

"*Antony and Cleopatra.*"

"It describes a world so immense that time yawns in it. We could discuss that, too."

THEY walk back to the campus. Professor Chalcott suddenly stops, and Fiona worries. "I find it difficult to talk when I'm on my pins," he says, seeing her concern. "A joke. Your Arab oil-producing new populace of London. An Arab rings up—an Arab with a good many women in his rented Georgian house—and says, 'This is your husband. To whom am I speaking?'"

Fiona says, "Jokes lighten the weight, don't they? The millstone on the chest in the middle of the night."

"You feel that weight?"

"Sometimes. Last night I was dreaming in dialogue, as usual, and woke myself up by speaking aloud but couldn't make myself hear myself because my throat was so dry."

"What did you get? A glass of water, or a pen?"

"A pen."

"That would have been my choice. Did the dialogue make sense in the morning?"

"Yes."

"What a folly, to ask such a question of you."

NEARLY at the college, Professor Chalcott takes her arm and says, "Shall we go and see *Long Day's Journey Into Night* this evening? It's a German company."

"Yes, please. Though you know I don't speak German."

He does not pull rank about the tickets. Their seats are very high up. Fiona keeps pausing on some pretext or other to give him a rest on the stairs. His hearing is bad. She has to attend carefully, though German is arcane to her, because he wants to know the details of the staging. She begins to feel like a guide dog for the blind: he can barely see. When the mother in the play comes downstairs to her suspicious family—she pacified by her secret fix of some drug—Chalcott knows by heart that the character must be carrying her wedding dress over her arms. "What does it look like?" he says.

"Cream tulle," says Fiona.

"No, I mean the way she's carrying it."

"Like a pile of freshly ironed fine laundry."

"A reviving idea, when the dress is old."

AGAIN, the next afternoon, he sits himself down heavily into the green plastic armchair in the library. He says, "Shall we go to see Dietrich tonight?"

"Live?"

"A swift scoot to New York?"

Fiona has already seen Dietrich in London, aeons ago, but a repetition would be worth it with him. "My right trusty and well-beloved friend" comes into her mind: the adjectives of English citations. And again she feels like a guide dog. She can repeat the English and the French to him; the German is once more a problem. The verbal information he wants in all languages has to be exact. Miss Dietrich is wearing her beautiful sequined body stocking. Professor Chalcott, that most distinguished and noticeable man, suddenly says, straining his eyes, finding that useless, and employing a loud voice, "Can you see her nipples?"

THERE lies between Professor Chalcott and Fiona a gentle, unexacting variation of humor and event. He appears brusque, but few people have ever sought to punish him. After the Dietrich evening, he takes Fiona back to her dormitory and they find Professor Krzyżowska on the door-step waiting for them. Fiona, knowing that violence makes Chalcott sick at heart, grasps his arm and steers him to his house. A tugboat guiding a great liner perhaps soon to be broken up, except that liners can be replaced by christening some new hulk *The Professor Chalcott II*, and there is no analogy for such a man as this. Fiona comes back to the dormitory. Professor Krzyżowska is still lurking. She says, "I must repeat myself. He's going to die first. You must protect yourself."

"We're on a doorstep," says Fiona. "Do you want to come up?"

"It's for your own good."

Fiona has a room to herself. She sits on the bed, Professor Krzyżowska in the only chair, a desk chair that reminds her of the backboard/blackboard confusion.

"You must see younger men," the Professor says.

"What are you trying to do? Are you in love with him?"

"I'm thinking of you. You should be going out with other students. A safeguard. I saw you taking him home. It's I who should have taken him home."

"You *are* jealous."

"You'll suffer."

"Self-protection hasn't much to do with friendship."

"I'm on my own," says the Professor, without meaning to.

"I know. I'm sorry."

"I'm going to *stop* this nonsense," the Professor shouts.

It can then go either way. Peril is in the room, the likelihood of real damage; or the Professor can be touched on the arm. Fiona chooses to brush her teeth.

"Why are you brushing your teeth?" The danger starts to disappear.

A pause. Fiona says, "Sorry, my mouth was full."

"I know some apt young men on this very campus."

"Why apt?"

"As I said. They're your age."

Fiona sits on the bed and then stands, feeling it wrong to slouch when the Professor's frame of mind beseeches respect.

"You see," says Fiona, trying yet once more, "I don't want to be with people of my own age all the time. Not just for the sake of it. I mean, I was trying to get someone my own age out of a trance in the library a while ago. I've never had to wake Professor Chalcott up. We have fun. I've never enjoyed myself so much with anyone. Are you saying that I'm in your way? Troubling you?"

"I wish you spoke Polish. All your Russian is no good to me. I abhor."

"Your English is perfect."

"No."

"You mean not fluent enough to say what's at the back of your mind?"

The Professor gets up and walks about the room to command it. Fiona says, "I don't understand the age-ghetto principle we have in America. I don't want to go around with some husky athlete just because he's nineteen."

"You'll see I'm right later."

"If one only knows one's contemporaries, how is the past to be handed on?"

"I'm talking about the inevitable loss. Guard against the future."

"But we're happy *now*."

"You can't afford this. It's against nature." The Professor goes over to the bed and yells, "Someone's been sleeping here!"

"Me."

Impasse. Fiona takes the Professor's chair, but sits on the arm of it. "You see, he is my *great* friend. How many great friends does anyone have in a lifetime, including husband and brothers and sisters and children and parents? Twelve? Fifteen? With luck. I'm not talking about acquaintances or well-wishers."

"I'm just telling you that you are laying yourself open." The Professor picks up a pencil and vents helpless anger by breaking the point off. "I suppose I should apologize for this," she says. "I'll get you another."

"The contagion of the world's slow stain," says Fiona.

"Who said that?"

"You did, once. You said it was Shelley," says Fiona. "A friend to you, and not even Polish. Certainly not your age. I wonder if I could get you something? The Coke machine's just down the corridor."

"A glass of ice water."

"It would have to be a paper cup."

The Professor throws the slept-on pillow out of the window.

THE next afternoon, Chalcott meets Fiona on campus and says, "Lot of swansdown outside your bedroom window."

"Professor Krzyżowska threw a pillow out of it."

Professor Chalcott drops his cane, bends down to get it, can't reach. "Would you mind picking up my cane?" Project achieved. "One of the things I like about you is that you wear dresses with waists," he says. "Also you remind me of Cleopatra. Interesting that you should have been reading that play. Shakespeare's, of course, not Shaw's. Shaw isn't very good at women. You're *very* good at it. At being one."

Fiona stays quiet. He goes on, taking her arm as they walk. "You always suggest something around yourself. The past. Beethoven carries Mozart around with him. Anyway, what was that woman doing, killing a swan outside your window?"

"I wasn't speaking loud enough. She wasn't killing a swan, she was thrashing around with my pillow. I think she thought you'd been lying on it. You can't blame her."

"I can and do."

THEY walk to his house. Chalcott says, "I'm eager to play you something I believe I may have deciphered from Beethoven's shorthand. I want to talk to you about whether you think I've got it right. Then I want to play you Cole Porter."

"Important about the shorthand."

"I nearly called you up in the middle of the night, but I

didn't think you'd welcome being woken. So after playing the piano, and having some sardines, I simply wrote out the idea on staff paper and imagined your being there."

"I was awake anyway. I nearly rang you to tell you something from an encyclopedia I was proofreading."

"Why proofreading?"

"It's one of the jobs on the bulletin board. I can think about better things in the back of my mind, so it's bearable. I get the encyclopedia free, too, but it's not up to much. I was going to read you an entry about the character they had as Friar Tuck in *Romeo and Juliet*. Friar Laurence turned into a Toby jug."

"I should say a researcher just chose the most familiar Friar."

THEY go later into a store where Professor Chalcott has tracked down a Virginia ham. Professor Krzyżowska is there and looks at them askance. She takes Fiona aside. "Virginia ham is too salt for him," she says. "You'll kill him, you and the Virginia ham."

"He wants me to taste it. He says it's the taste of his country as he remembers it at my age," says Fiona. "He was brought up in Virginia."

"A mistake, the salt, for his digestion."

"I don't think so," says Fiona.

Professor Chalcott appears from behind a smoked turkey and says, "Mistake?"

Professor Krzyżowska says, "The salt. At your age. Fiona shouldn't allow it."

"Bunk," says Professor Chalcott. "Fiona doesn't make mistakes." He leaves again to settle the bill. He thinks as he goes that some things one does seem correct but out of pitch, and that other things one does can seem errors but in pitch. Alone with the Polish Professor, Fiona says, "The point is, Virginia ham gives him pleasure."

# Fakt

"YOU look at things through the wrong end of a municipal drainpipe," said the Right Honorable Jerzy Szymanski over the dishwasher-stacking to his wife, Stephanie Perceval, who was a member of the Greater London Council.

"You rinse glasses ready for the dishwasher better than I do," she said fondly. "What do you mean, the wrong end of a municipal drainpipe?"

"Not seeing the wood for the trees."

"You do muddle metaphors. I suppose that would be Polish of you."

"No, it's me of me. We Poles are usually exact. What I meant was that you don't see how important it is, having received this invitation to go to what promises to be a very festive occasion in this Polish village that seems to remember me and where I have many cousins that I don't recall. I expect it was the later thoughts of you that blocked it all out. I remember you practicing the piano in your Portland Place flat in the second half of the War when I was a butler at the Government-in-Exile Embassy in Devonshire Street, facing your piano. You had the most beautiful hair. It was not a very good piano but you played Polish music. I used to wait at the door at eight-fifteen in the morning to watch you go off to school on your bike. Your music case bumped against your left ankle. You played the 'Polonaise' too fast."

"It's the same as about the pilmeni. I never do it quite right. I leave a mess on the plates."

"It comes off in the dishwasher if I rinse them first."

"That's making two operations of one. Like your calling yourself 'Szymanski' to M.P.s who can't say it and 'Standard' to Polish shoe menders who can."

"Is that why you go on calling yourself Perceval? To avoid the 'Szymanski' problem?"

"I'd call myself Szymanski in a second, but not Standard. Not something after a motor car. What would you think if Timothy suddenly decided to call himself Toyota?" Timothy was their son.

"Alvis would be a nice surname."

"You talk as if surnames were arbitrary."

"In Poland, everything is arbitrary. We've been used as a corridor for centuries. I'd like you to take me back to Poland. Would you? You've left bits of beetroot from the borscht in the blender, too. You'd have to force me to face Warsaw again. You speak better Polish than I do."

"We'd only be on our way to Russia. You don't mean to say you're scared of being held there without trial? Not as a *Junior Minister*. Wouldn't there be a big welcome for you? Dancing, vodka, recognitions? I thought that was the point?"

Jerzy studied the telegram. "It says it's from the village where I was born and that they want to do honor to . . ."

". . . An important," said Stephanie, leaning over his shoulder.

". . . English ally," said Jerzy, "and member of the Cabinet whom we wish to be honored in his birthplace. I wish I could remember it. All I can remember is Warsaw and the Uprising and the rebuilding of the Old Town. We copied it from paintings of Canaletto. We did it brick by brick rescued from the demolition we scrabbled through. Canaletto painted bricks very exactly."

"Why don't you want to come to Poland?"

"I'm frightened of going back alone. I don't even speak

Polish any longer. I can't make myself. So much lost."

"Yes you do. You speak it in your sleep. That's mostly how I've learned it. Of course you must go. I'll try to come. They're proud of you."

NEXT day, Jerzy had to go to a lunch at the Zoological Society. He was shown an experiment in which cats were exposed to a hiss of air that made their hair blow the wrong way. How to make a neurotic. His own fur seemed to have been blown the wrong way for too long, until he had met Stephanie.

His acute and young-voiced wife was persuaded to accept the invitation. She also rang an old Polish girlfriend of his called Kakia, whom Stephanie understood to have been his mistress, and arranged that the invitation should include her. Kakia had bouffant peroxided hair and an expression of fortitude and sweetness. Stephanie knew her to be a great support to her husband and she suppressed jealousy. Stephanie saw down a great deal more than a drainpipe. So did Kakia.

THEY arrived in Warsaw by airplane, to travel by car many miles. Jerzy was welcomed in English, spoken with difficulty, as "Mr. Standard." Many people said they remembered Kakia. No one knew Stephanie, though they were gratified by her speaking Polish. She chattered helpfully to the mayor. Flags were hanging out for this famous child of a small Polish village, this boy who had done so well in so famous a country as England. Jerzy, with ceremony and diffidence, signed the visitors' book. His wife hung back and gestured to Kakia, whose Western-looking hair was commented on with awe by the villagers. They were all three welcomed into small home after small home, where there were toasts to the ancient friendship between England and Poland. Until now, Jerzy had found himself unable to speak Polish: could merely understand it.

He seemed to recall almost nothing, though he thought he

remembered the postman, now seventy. He ransacked his mind for better than cruel memories. None of these meadows came back to him, none of these modest cottages. But his cousins all seemed to know him. He and Stephanie and Kakia were finally given beds in three separate cottages, after many more toasts and many piroskis and many adages. An elderly farmer got up unsteadily and said, drinking to Jerzy, "A potato in the ground dreams only of the vodka it will be made into." Opaque though it was, this remark struck a hopeful note. Kakia beamed; Stephanie shone. There was some struggle among the cousins, amidst their many memories of Jerzy's early brilliance, about whether Kakia should be persuaded to leave Jerzy alone with his important meditations about politics or whether they should share a bedroom. All the cousins clearly remembered the great man's affection for Kakia, his wife. In the confusion of vodka, Stephanie and Kakia had exchanged places.

NEXT morning, when everyone was as clearsighted as only vodka drinkers can be after such a night, there continued to be much talk of Jerzy's prowess as a child. His forgetfulness of his many relations was put down to a misleading modesty about his eminence that only a family history of centuries of living in a country used as an international corridor could have produced, as an English lawn is produced only by five-hundred years of mowing and rolling. There was more vodka at breakfast. Stephanie allowed Kakia and Jerzy to act out their parts as husband and wife. More and more relations turned up, producing photographs of themselves that they wanted Jerzy to autograph.

That evening there was a ball in the Town Hall. People were in a mood of gaiety that could have lasted for days: their home-town boy made good, with such a pleasant wife and such a quiet woman, too, probably his secretary. In the midst of the ball the mayor stopped the band.

"Ladies and gentlemen," he said, "I have to announce a

most awkward occurrence." He blew his nose. "A gentleman has arrived from England with the same famous name of Szymanski, also with his wife, and a charming helper. On consideration, we shall welcome him."

The village was united in not recognizing this new arrival as having anything to do with their past. The church officials had no memory of him. Nor had the school officials. He was a tank-shaped man equipped with a wife with the gangling gait of a Bloomsbury writer, and a mistress with hair more bouffant than Kakia's. People at the dance froze. The new Szymanski was recognized by no one. Stephanie lowered her voice, looking at the new mistress, and said helpfully to Jerzy of Kakia, "I like ours better."

Next day Jerzy, beside himself with the difficulty of it all, went off into the countryside to collect wild flowers with Stephanie. He was followed by a trail of people who counted themselves his proud cousins and told tales of promising audacity in his youth that they remembered well; oh, very well indeed. There had been a large fish caught when he was a mere boy. Early marks of fame to come. "And that's a fact," people repeated to one another in the Slav phrase for consolidating the vague. They spoke of the way he used to read studious foreign books when he was on school nature-study walks, always with this delicate habit of hiding behind trees and reading standing up. The new cardboard-box-of-an-imposter should be ignored. It was the only courteous thing to do.

The schoolmaster, looking proudly at Jerzy, said. "The men like this other visitor who go into politics now are like tailors. Not like *our* Jerzy. This decoy who has descended on us deserves a profession in letting out trousers."

To put things in order, the mayor allowed both men to sign the village visitors' book. He presented them both with the official order of merit, hastily made up, with Jerzy's name written both in Polish and in English and the other Jerzy's only in Polish. There should be some distinction between the men, even though the obvious fraud also spoke both languages. There was great frigidity on the part of the village people toward the interloper, great intimacy with the long-lost and famous cousin, who did not in fact remember anything of them at all, recalling only the dampness and rats in the sewers of Warsaw when he had been fighting as a boy in the underground.

But that was another matter. The tank-shaped man was, of course, the real original inhabitant, but his manners were less decorous, his memory less bereft. The point was the belief of the village in the son they proudly held to be theirs. Therein lay the fact.

# Timely Is the Hand That Winds the Clock

A BLAZING, balmy London summer day. Secretaries in blowing muslin dresses, eating sandwiches in the plaza off St. James's. Above them, in a small boardroom, an annual conference about Christmas-cracker mottoes. The question of Christmas-cracker mottoes had been merged with the question of the verbal innards of Chinese fortune cookies. A matter of contraction. Just as it was an unusually small conference room. The conference table could be folded up into a four-foot square at any moment, in case the room needed to be turned into a lettable flat for two. "For goodness knows what things are coming to," said the Chair.

The secretary, taking minutes, said, "'—what things are coming to.' I don't know, I'm sure." She spoke to no one, because no one there had for decades spoken to her, let alone by name. Some heard. Two, to be accurate. The Chair and a member called Alice, long in love with each other.

"Blimey, it's hot," said a Mr. Evershed. "Sorry. I should have addressed the Chair. Hot, Mr. Chairman."

The Chair said, in the person of Andrew J. J. Dupree, "Perfectly all right not to address the Chair. Let's open windows. Lovely day." He banged a small silver-plated gavel. "There's some water in front of us all but it's a trifle warm, because the fridge isn't working. All here, aren't we?"

He looked down the table at the annual faces. "It's urgent to
think Christmas, warm as we may be, Edwardian summers
and so on, *that* past not lost. Now." He drank some water,
warm indeed. "Christmas. That's what we're here for.
Blizzards, log fires, people clapping their hands around their
shoulders to keep warm, children with toboggans, porridge, a
nice lining to your stomach before your journey, shawls
doubled around babies' heads, coughs and sneezes spread
diseases."

Mr. Gaskell, one of the tried and trusted, blew his nose in
response to the last, a wartime slogan carried in public places.

Andrew said, "That's the spirit."

Mr. Gaskell raised his hand and said, "Before we get going,
might I ask the Chair, given the small license of all these
years, what do the Chair's initials, 'J. J.,' stand for?"

"We'll go into that later. As Other Matters on the agenda,
if you like." Andrew looked at his watch. "To work." He
glanced down the table toward the only woman contributor,
Alice, who was writing a note on a pad. What a mind, he
thought. Always working. It was a mind he had known and
loved for many years, but he was not a man to push things
too far. For twenty years, give or take a year or two, Alice's
loyalty to her husband, elsewhere, had prevented more than
meetings such as these and occasional dinners. He passed her
a folded note down the table: "I believe Boulestin might be
able to dig up some *fraises des bois* if I organized it. Are you
free? At 8:15?" He always went through such courtesies. In
the meantime, Alice had passed her note, also folded over, to
Mr. Gaskell: "About 'J. J.' Would you very much mind
dropping it?"

Mr. Gaskell read that and passed another note, open, down
the table, reading, "Alice. Why?"

A Mr. Morton held up his hand. "A suggestion for a
Christmas-cracker riddle for the under-ten category. I see it
in the more expensive range of cracker. Such a cracker would
include, say, a diamond ring—fake, of course—a paper hat, a
very small pack of playing cards, some further memento or

present, and the riddle (or joke): 'Q. What is the difference between your overcoat and a baby? A. One you wear, the other you was.'"

"I don't understand it," said a Mr. Bishop, a small man with ruddy cheeks, who looked like a coachman on a Christmas card.

At the same time, Alice was passing back to Mr. Gaskell the answer to his "Why?" on a new folded piece of paper: "I believe 'J. J.' refers to name in ghastly poem about small boy (A. A. Milne). The Chair wishes to gloss over his mother's lapse. 'James James,' between you and me and the gatepost. Natural enough in the case of a mother with a new baby, but names not fitting to the Chair. Though they may explain his perception about people's predicaments. People such as children."

"This riddle or joke of Mr. Morton's," said Andrew, wondering what Alice had been writing. "It takes a little puzzling over, but children like that. I suggest we take a vote. It should be limited to the *eight-to-ten*-year-old category of cracker, in my opinion, because of the question raised in a putative five-year-old's mind about 'the other you was.' In case he or she doesn't yet know the difference between the tenses, you see."

Mr. Gaskell said, "He or she certainly wouldn't," cracking his fingers.

Alice said, "I think, Mr. Gaskell, with the permission of the Chair to speak directly, that a five-year-old is likely to be rather acutely aware that he *was* a baby. Proud of it, you see. That it's done with."

Discussion was held. A vote was taken. The riddle, or joke, was taken down by the secretary as passed, for the five-to-eight-year-old category in the upper price range of crackers.

The mottoes for Christmas crackers began to pour in on pieces of paper. "Q. Why is a pig's tail like a carving knife? A. Because it's waved over ham."

"I believe that's a Victorian one," said a Mr. Wren, a man

well read in such things. He rarely came up with a riddle but was to be trusted on origins.

"Good riddles always last," said a Mr. Lassell. "Think of 'Q. When is a door not a door? A. When it's a jar.' That's given many of us a good time."

"We've had that since the year dot," said Mr. Morton.

"But there's always a new generation," said Andrew.

This riddle was postponed for the annual meeting two years hence, by which time, claimed Mr. Gaskell, the number of eight-year-olds new to the joke would have risen by 25 percent. The secretary, giggling a little, and possibly weeping a little as well, it being difficult to tell because of the steam on her spectacles, made a note and said to no one in particular, "Well, I've been here since the year dot and no doubt will be till I'm dot-and-carry-one, and I still think it's funny."

"The year dot, and dot-and-carry-one," said the Chairman, briefly putting his hand on her shoulder. "There's a germ of a joke there."

"I haven't the faintest idea what dot-and-carry-one means," said a well-versed American buyer named Mr. Ellis.

Andrew explained for the sake of the secretary. "It means elderly. Peg-legged, perhaps. At any rate, very, very old, and a pretty old phrase, I believe."

"It wouldn't do for the export market," said Mr. Ellis.

Andrew made a sign meaning "Don't be crushing." Mr. Ellis, a responsive man, smiled at the secretary and said, "No doubt it's a phrase we Americans should get to know. There's a real need for it." A glance immediately passed between Andrew and Alice, and both thought of their abiding place for each other. "Thank you," said Mr. Ellis to the secretary. Andrew was passed a folded note from Alice. "*Fraises des bois* would be a celebration indeed. But it really doesn't matter if Boulestin can't rustle them up. 8:15."

More and more riddles. At least 50 percent were vetoed as being dependent on the presence or otherwise of mothers with an explanatory turn of mind, which led to the annual discussion of whether the price of the costly cracker implied a mother without work to do. No one on this committee was witless about élitism in relation to Christmas crackers or any other matters. Alice rapidly wrote a number of riddles, passed them to Andrew, and said, "Mr. Chairman, we seem to have found through the years that our riddles are exclusively for children. Not mothers."

"What about the many *au pair* girls now who've been making the jellies and the sandwiches and who don't speak English very well?" asked Mr. Gaskell.

"The children will explain," said Alice.

"The all-important thing is that the cracker itself should go off. The dynamite thing inside," said Mr. Morton.

"It's the *non*-dynamite you're speaking of," said the Chair. "Nothing dangerous. Our pull thing depends on an element we've perfected that makes a harmonious bang. Nothing unsafe enters into it. I thought we all knew that to be a company policy." Everyone did. Even, upon thought, Mr. Morton, who felt himself an ass.

Alice said, "I think the problem is that children, small children, can't pull hard enough, and they screw the paper round in despair instead of tugging."

Andrew once again looked at Alice and made a note to himself to go into the question of paper quality. "And all shall be well and all manner of thing shall be well," he said.

Mr. Morton said, "I don't get that one."

Andrew said, "It's a quotation."

"Puck? Ariel?" said Mr. Bishop, the Christmas-coachman-cheeked member. "I'm eager to know."

"Eliot. T. S. Eliot," said Andrew.

"I believe it's 'Little Gidding,'" said Alice.

"Heavens," said Mr. Morton, cross with others' collusion when his cracker-pulling point had been flouted. "Heavens alive, we haven't even got to the fortune cookies yet. Mr. Chairman, couldn't we shut the windows and turn on the air-conditioning?"

"There's an energy crisis," said Andrew. "Pretty soon it'll

be a crisis about the need for people to be plain energetic."

"We'll be done in half an hour," said Mr. Bishop.

"Fortune-cookie suggestions," said the Chair, looking at Alice.

"What about 'Your next year will include travel and a love relationship'?"

Everyone found this excellent. Mr. Morton, acceding, closed his eyes and said, "Chop suey, nightlights to keep the food hot, dimmed lamps, *lovely*. It would suit whichever of the couple opened the cookie. I daresay it would be passed from hand to hand. Between the two. The two people, not the two hands of the one person." His pedantry was soft-voiced and had an honorable tone.

Mr. Gaskell suggested "He who toils will reach the top," but it was felt that this struck the wrong note for the end of a hardworking customer's day. And there was also the problem of the "he."

Alert as lay within his grasp, Mr. Morton said, "Well, then, what about 'He who looks outward and sees others is on the way to looking inward'?"

"Same problem, isn't it," Andrew said carefully. "I see the wisdom of course. The 'he' problem, though."

"Oh, Lord," said Mr. Morton, "I never enjoy this part. When it comes to contributing."

"Ah, no no no," said Mr. Bishop. "I mean, I enjoy listening to your ideas."

"I noticed you writing something," said Andrew to Mr. Bishop.

"It's not up to much," said Mr. Bishop. A pause. No one wished to interrupt. Young voices in love floated through the window from below. The pause extended. "'Happiness does not lie in restraint from grief,'" said Mr. Bishop.

Again a pause. This surprising man. Hands were raised in unity. Mr. Morton recovered from jealousy and tore up his own "Root out buzzards of sin which are coming home to roost."

Alice opened a folded note from Andrew that read "F.d.b. achievable. Already made sure this morning." She folded the note and put it in her bag. Looking round the table, she said, "I believe the 'he' thing isn't a hurdle. After all, it is a dinner for a couple we're thinking of. A man and woman. Fond, I mean."

Mr. Bishop was given the Chair's permission to ask her to go on. "If you could elaborate?" he said. She shook her head. Mr. Morton said, "If I may speak directly to our fellow-member as Alice after all these years, I suppose the reason for my blunders as to 'he' was that I woke up thinking, 'Two men looked through prison bars, one saw mud, the other stars.' The two men being anyone, you see. It's not good poetry, of course. It shouldn't go into the minutes. I must leave you for the moment, Mr. Chairman. A breath of air."

AT Boulestin, where the huge wall mirror is so old that no one ever catches himself—herself—looking at a reflection, where the ceiling is a dark brownish-red a little like bull's-blood marble, Andrew and Alice met promptly at eight-fifteen that evening. They talked to the waiters, who all knew them well. The restaurant was carpeted and quiet. So far as either of them had ever been able to tell, no one came here in a hurry, and it seemed that no one was ever here for the first time. There was a sense of order, restorative, upholding the waiters' long-lived affection for them. But after that, after the shrimp-and-rack-of-lamb discussions, Andrew was able to ask why she was shaking.

"Because of the meeting, I expect. It's always full of event, isn't it?" Alice paused, thinking of their exchange of notes, as he was. Nothing was said. They were not effusive. They never had been. Each went over the meeting without talking about it, until the first course came and Andrew said, "I suppose this job *is* worth doing, is it?"

"No question of it." But she was still shaking, and Andrew again asked why. "I'm frightened."

"For the umpteenth time, leave your husband and marry me."

"It would kill him."

"He'd survive. We have such a fine time."

"He died two months ago."

What to say.

"And I didn't tell you, Andrew, and even now I can't marry you."

"Explain why not."

"Later. Or do you want us to leave?" she said.

"I knew something had happened. I was going to ask you tonight."

"You're not eating," she said.

To carry a forkful of food to his mouth seemed the least he could do.

"That's better," she said.

"I'm so sorry," Andrew said, and then, to himself, "There was no need to say that." Platitudes, truisms, clichés all day, and now another awkwardness about to spring from his tongue. "Tell me," he heard himself commanding her, as if at a board meeting, "What would you say were the cardinal virtues?"

"You can't expect me to be a fortune cookie off duty." Hell, why even eat this dinner? "Mind Mr. Manners," she said to herself out loud, and Andrew looked round for this possible friend of hers, after all this time still not recognizing her habit of self-admonition.

He said, "I can't get into your head. It's the first time."

"I've stuck to you and I haven't let you down and I've got the right to shut up and I don't ask for more and I settled for it long ago. Just you try being a fortune cookie for one go, let alone all these years. Just you try being the Christmas cracker that doesn't pull. I've just thought of a riddle. 'Q. Where does a masochist live? A. In a basement.' Abasement."

Andrew thought, This woman has one sort of genius, a genius of the common tongue, and no one has ever told her so. "You do know what you can do, I suppose?"

"Nothing much."

"You can do anything. You could even reel off the seven deadly virtues."

"To fatuity," she said. She raised her glass at herself, and he raised his to her. "This unfortunate best-selling thought offered itself to me this morning," she said. "'Your fortune includes much travail.' Have you got a busy day tomorrow?" He laughed, and she said, "Why on earth are you laughing?"

"The cardinal virtues you won't tell me about. I thought, Damn, and now you'll make *me* say them because you've just proved them."

"Go on. Risk it."

He put some extra shrimps on her plate, knowing that she liked them, and she looked at them as if they were ink-pen octopus.

"Candor, valor, grace, humor," he said. "Darling, do try not to be a bitch. You know how I hate abstract nouns. And you made me do four in a row, but the trouble is that you demonstrate them."

She said, "Lessons in stones, and grammar in running brooks or whatever it is. You left one cardinal virtue out. *Mind.* The *cardinal* abstract virtue, and a *five*-year-old would aspire to it. In private, of course."

"They've got their place, I suppose. Abstract nouns."

"My rotten best-seller motto," she said. "Given your approval of it, and you did nod, and given 'travail,' what about 'Your next year will include travel and a love relationship'?" One for risks herself.

"I thought maybe the Loire this month. I want to know why we can't get married now."

"If you're going to ask me to paddle a canoe with you down the Loire, I'll scream."

"No, by car, and why aren't you answering me about why we can't get married?"

"Because we're too used to the way things are, I suppose.

Because something's calcified by now." He shook his head vehemently at this woman, always an amazement, but she plowed on: "Because we *have* had such a fine time for so long and I don't want it to stop."

"You're frightened of being demanding."

"So?"

"It's an act of trust to be demanding now and then."

"And this is a then and now."

She left a lot of shrimps, went to the telephone to think, dialed 123 for the time with the instinct to give herself time. She set her watch—the mainspring to be seen to, another burden on top of being asked to get married—and came back to the *fraises des bois*, laughing at all such excuses for feeling put upon. The *fraises* were delicate and costly. "About these cardinal virtues," she said. "I'm not very candid, am I, you see? About the dying, for instance. And I'm not at all brave. I've brooded about selling you short. And now I'm just plain furious that I didn't tell you about my husband. You could have *helped*. Also, things can't have stopped being as usual. Also, we could have lived together."

"Perhaps if one approaches a decision from behind—"

"Taking it by surprise—"

THEY lived together in great happiness. Alice went on refusing to get married. A baby was impossible, they both thought, without speaking of it, because when Alice was very young she had had children, now at the Sorbonne, and Andrew felt she shouldn't be encumbered with another generation to bring up. They rescued a cat of superior wit from a farmyard. His mother was dead, and he was six weeks old. They fed him with an eyedropper on watered milk and he clung to one of Andrew's leather motoring gloves on the sideboard, taking the glove for his mother. As he put on a few ounces, the kitten became clearly highborn, as the vet substantiated: an unusual mixture of Siamese and Burmese. Andrew and Alice, robbed of so much past that they might have had together, tended to think of him anthropo-morphically as one another. Alice held that he fled the room when anything but early keyboard music was playing and that he particularly hated opera. Andrew held that, being a cat, he was simply exercising options.

One morning, at five, Alice was lying awake quietly, being the quicker at finishing with sleep. She lay for twenty minutes. The cat, being hungry for breakfast and ignoring the dark in order to protect his right of choice, entered the bedroom meticulously and sat in an armchair. Andrew moved, obviously awake

"Oh, good. Are you awake?" said Alice.

"I didn't know you were awake," said Andrew.

"I've been awake for ages listening to you being awake and trying not to disturb you because you were trying not to disturb me, thinking I was asleep."

"There's that night gone," said Andrew.

"It's the morning. We can have coffee now."

"And feed the blithering cat."

"I said from the beginning that you were best alone."

She was already half dressed. Andrew followed, doing as well as he might, but something fell over the day, like the wing of a large black bird blotting out the sun.

Andrew and Alice planned, separately, both hating public holidays, a non-Christmas morning with crackers and Chinese mottoes. Sometime—a warm autumn day before non-Christmas—Alice said to Andrew in the kitchen, "I wonder what happens to unanswered questions."

"Where are my Grape-Nuts? And what do you mean?"

"You remember our secretary last summer?"

"Of course."

"What did she mean? I asked her after the conference and she didn't know."

"Asked her what?"

"What she meant by saying, 'I don't know, I'm sure,'"

Andrew found his Grape-Nuts, fed the cat, went into

another room to play the clavichord. After a while, and with the balance of the instrument's docility, he came back into the room to reply, "I daresay she meant she wasn't sure she knew."

"That would be something quite different."

"You do ponder."

The cat sat daintily, poised for exits, watching.

Alice went on, "I *more* daresay she meant she was in soggy terrain where she couldn't find her feet. Sandy, perhaps. Sand hills changing shape in the desert because of the wind at night. She meant she *knew* that she wasn't *sure*. Obliquely to what you said." In the kitchen, she threw a cup into the sink and broke off the handle. The cat ran away, in flight from chaos.

SOME later and colder non-Christmas day, Andrew and Alice were opening their Christmas crackers as their common surprise for each other. Each had made a tray for the other laden with small presents. They had each been waiting for the other to wake up and each been delighted at concealed dawn awareness, though Andrew mustered a touch of grumpiness. And then the cat, still very young, limped into the room as if only from a long sleep in a cupboard of sweet-smelling sheets. It was Alice who found that his feet were raw with walking. Who knew what he had lived on. The cat played with the tissue paper and the mottoes. Andrew played the clavichord. The cat, knowing tact, moved between one and the other of his owners. Alice shouted, "I think he's come back because of the tissue paper."

"No, because of my clavichord."

"He can't hear it because of the racket of the tissue paper. There's a *new* motto here. 'Great men were gods, if beggars could not kill 'em.' Andrew, did you allow that nonsense? What would a five-year-old make of that? What do I make of it?"

Andrew came back and said, "Something's missed out of the list of cardinal virtues."

"Attention," she said.

"*I'd* been thinking that. Where do you think the cat was? I daresay he wrote that motto when he was asleep in your feather boa."

"No," said Alice, "his paws are raw. He's ravenous."

Andrew went to the kitchen and came back with the chicken livers fried in butter on a saucer.

"Once done, done forever. You'll have to be feeding him on chicken giblets every morning now," said Alice, handling a replica of an Egyptian burial hippopotamus that he had given her.

"You said, 'Once done, done forever.' To wake up on non-Christmas to a living Christmas-cracker motto!"

"But the cat did come back on the right day," said Alice. She bathed the cat's paws, and put him to sleep with a pillow between him and the light, and stuffed the non-Christmas chicken, and put an alarm clock into her jacket pocket to remind her when the chicken would be cooked. She went out, saying that she was going out, uttering the deducible. Andrew kissed her, drew the curtains for the cat's sake, and sat down in the library.

Alice rang up later from a telephone box.

"Where the hell are you?" he said.

"In a telephone box. Is the chicken done?"

"You should know. You should be here. Why is an alarm going off? Are you in a fire engine?"

"The chicken's done. Could you take it out?"

"You've walked somewhere, haven't you? Yes, the oven. Are you all right? Where are you?"

"Go on talking."

"A virtue we left out," he said, but her coin ran out. Constancy, thought Andrew. Constancy, thought Alice as she walked the considerable way to the house. "Thank you," she said to Andrew.

AGAIN Andrew took Alice to Boulestin. Venison was in season. He had bought her a brooch of gold, which he took out of his watch-fob pocket and pinned onto her jacket.

"It's a very small brooch," he said, disappointed in it. She unclasped it carefully and balanced it on several fingers. "But a very big ring," she said. He concentrated on trivia, and said that she hadn't tasted the venison.

"Because of the brooch, you see. Or ring," she said.

"It could very easily be turned into a ring. I asked the jewelry man in case the same flighty thought occurred to you. Only in case." He disliked his talk, and said, "You haven't read the note." He had had something printed, as if for a Christmas cracker or a fortune cookie. The expense, she thought; and the trouble, greater. Some pale-yellow flowers and mauve violets of carefully sincere poverty of feeling had been printed to circle the words. The design suggested scented chocolates. The motto said, "A hungry belly hath no ears." It had the tiger spring of the totally meaningless.

"Good," she said.

"I'm glad it passes." He was looking not at the motto but at the brooch still balanced on her fingers. "I'm afraid it's only a small number of carats." She looked at him in the particular way she had when she was on the verge of nonsense promising sagacity, and said, though as if to the card of the earless belly, "It's not the thought, it's the words that count."

It took him a while to gather her meaning. "And another of the same," she said. "Never trouble trouble until trouble troubles you."

"A motto run amok among the U.N. simultaneous translators would bring alertness to the world."

# In Trust

## Melinda    Gavin
## Kate

ACT I

We are in a small cobbled street leading into a square of cream-painted Georgian houses, all alike, with columns beside the front steps. Perspective view of one side of the square and of a few distant houses at the far corner. It is a quarter to eight in the evening of some balmy night in the nineteen-sixties. Street lamps along the square. We can also see, running parallel to the big houses, behind them, a cobbled mews of tiny houses, not well kept up: houses that used to serve as stables and grooms' quarters for each of the big houses.

Melinda and Gavin are in their early fifties, but played by actors whose ages are noncalculable. Only their faces are lighted. They are sitting outside a pub with their granddaughter, Kate—seven going on eight, with obvious confiding fondness for her grandparents. Played by an adult actress: an augury of what the little girl is going to be. Spotlight on her face, too. Head level therefore lower than her grandparents'. Her hair is in pigtails, and we can just see the top of her sailor suit. She is slumped in her chair. Glasses in front of them on a white wrought-iron round table under a parasol, one of three outside the pub. A little light comes from the pub's open door. The only other light is thrown through the stained-glass window of the church at the near end of the square. The church has been opened for someone to practice the organ. We hear the organ often, faintly. Cars occasionally.

\* \* \*

MELINDA (*to Kate, raising glass*): Happy birthday, darling. In anticipation. Another month.

KATE: I've been seven for ages and ages. It never stops.

GAVIN: For someone who has recently learned to talk, like you, the years between one and three must have seemed a millennium.

KATE: I've talked ever since I can remember.

MELINDA: You see up the mews there, darling? Those are old coach houses.

KATE: As old as you?

GAVIN: About four times as old.

KATE: Good Christ.

MELINDA (*to Gavin, quietly*): At least she said "good." (*To Kate*) Anyway, darling, the mews houses. We can see that at the minute they'd look more your scale, but we're thinking of the future. They sell for much less than our house, the house we're going to give you later. We're keeping it up for you so that we can leave you something that will last.

GAVIN: Family tiara.

KATE: Where will you be?

MELINDA: Hanging on somewhere.

GAVIN (*to Kate*): Popped off. Kicked the bucket.

(*Melinda makes "no" gesture to Gavin.*)

GAVIN (*to Kate*): If you'd been a boy when you were born, we'd have laid down a pipe of port.

KATE: A harbor?

GAVIN: No, a drink for later.

KATE: *Later!*

GAVIN: We decided to put the house in trust for you even before you were born, and we guessed right, because Mummy really lives in it in her head, which is why she keeps all her books there. She's sometimes away earning money for you to go to university and your quitter Daddy will love you later but not until he's put in his dog-discipline water-school.

KATE: Good Christ.

GAVIN (*to Melinda*): There it is again.

KATE: Why does he need the dog thing when he's got a lake? Is he still in Derbyshire?

GAVIN: Yes.

MELINDA: Some people like a lot of water. At different temperatures. The dog-discipline school is kept at seventy-nine degrees.

KATE: How do you know?

MELINDA: He said so in the papers.

KATE: He never writes to me.

MELINDA: He sent you a bikini for Christmas.

KATE: I keep trying, but I can't fit it.

GAVIN: And he'll put in riding stables, perhaps. You must be braced for riding stables.

MELINDA: And he'll put in a gym, perhaps.

KATE: Jumping over the rope still scares me, but I'm good on the parallel bars and I like the ribs.

MELINDA: Your hair would float when you're upside down. You've been upside down a lot lately. I've noticed. Since your hair's grown.

GAVIN: On the fire-escape ladder in your day nursery.

KATE: My hair feels nice. (*Throughout this act, she keeps undoing one pigtail or the other and lets the hair brush against her neck, wriggling herself to and fro.*) Could I have a fountain pen? Why doesn't Daddy send me a fountain pen?

GAVIN: We'll get you one. We did actually get you one last Christmas, but you didn't want it.

KATE: The school confiscated it. They said I made too much mess with the blotting paper at the bottom of the inkwell.

GAVIN: Why is there blotting paper at the bottom of your inkwell?

KATE: I expect a lot of younger children put it there. And then it collects on the bottom of your pen and you can flick the glub at the Scripture mistress. Also they say a fountain pen's bad for your handwriting. It's not. Only if you make a mess. Then it's harder to rub out than pencil, of course. Quite often you rub it out so hard that you make a hole in the paper and then have to start all over again. *But not if you have ink eradicator.*

MELINDA: What's ink eradicator?

KATE: It's in two bottles in a box with instructions. I buy it with my pocket money. You're not supposed to do ink eradicating, so you follow the instructions with your desk flap up on your head. First you apply No. 1 and the mess looks even worse and you don't despair and you blow on it until it looks hopeful, and then you put on No. 2 and the whole thing disappears except that then you have to go on waiting until it's all dry or else there's *another* mess.

GAVIN (*to Melinda*): Children are much at the mercy of their equipment.

KATE: What about this gym of Daddy's?

GAVIN: He's proud of his figure. He buys very expensive clothes. So far he hasn't given much thought to you since he ran out on your mother. We thought it was best to explain to you in confidence now that you're older. Do you know what "in confidence" is?

KATE: Yes.

GAVIN: We mean, to explain why we're your parents, really. And about the point of the house. Your Mummy put up a horizontal ladder over the nursery staircase. Hung with Japanese paper lampshades and jingling glass from Czechoslovakia and many other beautiful things. Just before you were born.

KATE: I doubt if I could do it.

(*She stands up on the chair with her arms up, as if to hammer, and can't.*)

MELINDA (*after a glance at Gavin*): Would you like a sausage, Kate?

KATE: Yes, please. I've got some money, Granny. I shook it out of my money bank that Daddy gave me. There were seven pennies and a farthing.

MELINDA: Thank you, but the sausage is a present. *(Disappears out of sight.)*

GAVIN: Did the money come out easily?

KATE: I just banged it out.

GAVIN: Oh dear, your Daddy gives you a lot of toys that don't quite work. No point in beating around the bush.

KATE: Could you beat around a tree?

GAVIN: The bush is there for alliteration. B–b. Like "neither fish, flesh, nor fowl." Like "Mickey Mouse." Like "chatty children."

*(Kate falls silent.)*

GAVIN: I *like* chatty children.

KATE: Where's Granny?

GAVIN: Getting the sausage.

KATE: We could split it into three.

*(Melinda comes back with the sausage. Kate splits it into three.)*

MELINDA: You see the back street behind the square?

KATE: Behind your house?

MELINDA: It's really your house, as we said. It's in trust for you.

KATE: What *does* that mean?

MELINDA: Being kept for you later.

KATE: Everything is later. I wanted to get a sausage here on the way back from feeding the ducks, and the people in the pub said nothing could be sold to me until later.

MELINDA: To go back to the coach houses.

MELINDA: What coach houses?

KATE: Those little houses. They used to be used for horses.

KATE: Could I have a horse?

MELINDA: I'd rather not.

KATE: Why?

GAVIN: Your Mummy broke her collarbone on a horse we liked.

KATE: How old was she?

GAVIN: About twenty. It healed.

KATE: How old are you now?

GAVIN: It doesn't matter.

MELINDA: Of course it does, at her age.

KATE: How many cousins have I got?

MELINDA: Gavin?

GAVIN: No first cousins.

KATE: Why?

GAVIN: Your Mummy and your Daddy hadn't got any brothers or sisters.

KATE: Like me.

GAVIN: But you've got a lot of great-aunts and great-uncles. Granny's and my brothers and sisters.

KATE: How many?

GAVIN: Granny is one of eight children and I'm one of eleven, so that's seventeen.

KATE: Are they as old as you?

GAVIN: Some older, some younger.

KATE: What are you drawing?

GAVIN: A family tree.

KATE: Put in their birthdays. Oh yes, I know Stephen. He's the one who ate a whole fried egg at breakfast. In one swallow. Also he jumped all over his bed squashing mosquitoes with his pillow. The old Nanny thought it was me.

MELINDA: That was why I sacked her. I knew it was him. It didn't matter.

KATE: Tell me how you and Granddaddy met.

GAVIN: We met on a tennis court. I was playing with my first cousin and he had a friend coming over, a girl, and she said could she bring her cousin. That was Granny.

KATE: Then what?

GAVIN: Then we got married, and three years later we had our first quarrel, and I said to her, Oh, go and put your head in the loo, and I went and looked for her and she had her head in the loo, and that was when I fell in love with her.

MELINDA: Do you want another sausage?

KATE: Describe the house as if I've never seen it. I haven't,

really. The old Nanny said I'm in the maids' floor, as if that
was bad. So does the new one.

GAVIN: *(to Melinda)*: Another one who'll have to go. *(To
Kate)* In that case, you're coming down to sleep in the
dressing room. You could do me a favor and sleep on the
dressing-room bed and press my trousers underneath the
mattress while you sleep.

MELINDA: Well, this house. Shut your eyes. There's a
garden in the middle of the square. It has cherry blossom and
apple blossom. There's a very old oak tree where you used to
swing, but the swing's hung too low for you now. Only the
people in the square have keys to the garden. I've just today
bought you this chain with your key on it.

*(Kate takes the chain carefully.)*

KATE: It looks like gold. Gold bends if you bite it, the
science mistress says. *(She bites the chain.)* Yes, it bent.

GAVIN: What the hell sort of school is this?

MELINDA: Now you go up four steps, between columns
painted pale cream, with four figures at the tops. The ones
we had done in white.

KATE: Six, Granny. There are two more figures on the
ceiling of the alcove by the lanterns.

MELINDA: Then you put your key into the door. You go
along a corridor made of gray slate that Granddaddy and I got
in Wales. Off that corridor there is a huge dining room, for
the most splendid parties you could imagine. A long refectory
table where monks used to sit hundreds of years ago, and
twenty brown leather chairs with old brass studs that date
from the days of Cromwell, and at the head and the foot two
paler brown chairs from Spain that a king and a queen used to
sit in. Your Granddaddy and I had two copper doors,
eighteen foot high, especially made for the dining room. It
didn't cost very much then, because Granddaddy was an art
student. The whole house didn't cost very much. When your
Mummy brought you back from hospital, everyone in the
house was so pleased that they leaned over your cradle, which

your Mummy had beside her chair. Your Daddy sat at the other end of the table, but it was too far away and he came and sat beside you. Then your Granddaddy and I went up into the morning room to listen to the gramophone, and you seemed to like the harpsichord records best and in a very few minutes you went to sleep. *(Melinda brings out a penny whistle and plays five notes.)* Can you hear that there's a different space between two of the notes?

KATE: The third and the fourth.

MELINDA: It's called a semitone. The others are tones. The fifth note is called the dominant. I think you're going to be musical. I always did. Oh, I forgot to tell you, there are fairy lights all along the big dining-room lighting fixture. Your Daddy had thought of it, and he put them in himself. You moved your arms at them. Your Mummy had got thin, but you should have seen the lunch she had. The cook thought she wouldn't want anything, but she suddenly said she'd been wanting bacon and eggs for months but hadn't felt hungry.

KATE: After that, was I ever properly in the dining room as a child?

GAVIN: Your Mummy gave a birthday party for you when you were two. She asked us because we'd given her the house as a wedding present in trust for you. Your Daddy was very nice and gave us the cottage at the bttom of the garden until we moved in to look after things when he'd gone.

KATE: After the morning room, then what happens?

MELINDA: More stairs, and the drawing room. Your Granddaddy and I bought you some doves the day you were born, and you used to lie there listening to them.

KATE: They're still there, aren't they?

GAVIN: Of course. *(Pause)* Sometimes they die, but we get new ones.

MELINDA: Then you can skip the next two floors, because they're not much fun apart from a big bath in the middle of a room. You'll grow into it. Then there are the library and the study, and then your nurseries. Mummy had a gate put up at the very top of the stairs, with a blackboard on one side for you to draw on.

KATE: That gate isn't there now.

MELINDA: We had it taken away. You didn't seem to like it. And we thought you might want to let the floor when you own it. It was meant for you when you were a baby.

KATE: I've still got my eyes shut, but dreams are very tiring. Could I have another sausage? Will you?

GAVIN: Granny's on a diet.

KATE: What's that?

GAVIN: Later, again.

KATE: Everything's later again.

MELINDA: What we're worried about is inflation. Not the way I've got bigger—I come and go—but how much the house may cost to keep up when you inherit it.

ACT II

*Four years later. Kate is eleven going on twelve. The same London pub, the same parasol. The same time of summery evening. Soprano voices from the same old church rehearsing Handel's "Ode for St. Cecilia's Day." Gavin and Melinda have again brought Kate out to have a drink with them before dinner. Noises of cars going by: more of them than in Act I. Kate, when we catch a glimpse of her below face level because of the dipped car headlights, is wearing jeans and a most English school blazer.*

GAVIN (*to Kate*): Sausage?

KATE: Haven't they got frankfurters?

GAVIN: Doubt it.

MELINDA: Darling, frankfurters aren't good for people anyway.

GAVIN: Made of horses' eyeballs.

KATE: Where could you get us one? I've never had eyeballs.

MELINDA: I expect Granddaddy was making it up. Something he'd read.

KATE: He doesn't do that. Elsie told me she gives him her

*Daily Mirror* when she comes to work every day after he's finished the *Times,* and he's always polite and always reads it but always says you can't believe a thing you read. She agrees, though they both read a terrific lot, don't they? Why does Elsie only come in for the evenings now?

MELINDA: It's because of what we were saying to you about inflation. Everything's going up.

KATE: And of course you keep on having to get me a new blazer.

MELINDA: Your Mummy pays for that. She always wants to know how tall you are.

KATE: Where is she exactly?

GAVIN: Russia.

KATE: Still?

GAVIN: Things take a long time in Russia.

KATE: Things take forever everywhere. What's she doing exactly now?

GAVIN: She's dancing and she's writing poetry. Do you write poetry much?

KATE: Only sometimes.

GAVIN: Do you find the house a good place to do it?

KATE: I mostly do it in the cupboard outside your bedroom. The one with the Hoover and my toys from when I was young. Sometimes in your library when you're not using it, but you are, generally.

MELINDA: Does your cat come in with you? Into the cupboard?

KATE: Course.

GAVIN: What's your favorite place in the house?

KATE: Your floors and the library and the cupboard. I don't much like the nursery floors. Everything's been moved around.

MELINDA: That's the Tennents.

KATE: They're very nice, of course. They keep asking me up and showing me the things you gave me when I was born. *(Confidentially)* There's one rotten thing they've done, and that's lost the key to the brass watch. The one that's like a clock, at the top of the nursery stairs. They keep saying they'll get a new one, but they always forget. Could I have a slumber party?

MELINDA: What?

KATE: A sleep-over?

GAVIN (*to Melinda*): It's an American phrase. There are a lot of American children in the square. No harm would come of it.

KATE: I hate people who hate Americans. My second-best friend comes from Arkansas. It's spelled like Kansas, but you say Arkansaw. My first-best friend comes from the Philippines and the Bronx. One parent from each.

MELINDA: Where would you like the slumber party?

KATE: Oh, in the drawing room, of course. I like the big rooms best now.

MELINDA: I heard you playing the clavichord with Mr. Juniper when he was tuning it.

KATE: But he was saying the delight of his life was the harpsichord. Could we have a Cornish pasty?

(*Gavin disappears into the pub. Kate draws a plan of the drawing room on the back of a china plate with a felt-tipped pen.*)

KATE: Elizabeth and John and Philip can sleep on the leather sofa. Patricia and Pamela and Derek can sleep on the velvet sofa. Eight more can sleep on the cushions in the alcove. Peter and Christopher and me can sleep on the gray sofa, except that I'll have to remember to move the Chinese cups on the table or Peter will bust one of them. He's a very good rower, and he rows in his sleep. That's seventeen. Jenifer with one *n* can sleep by the fireplace, and Jennifer with two *n*'s can sleep under the glass table. There'll probably be a few more. Donovan said he would come if he could sleep in Granddaddy's library with Claire. We've all got sleeping bags, and I'll wake everyone up because we've got to deal with the problem of getting Candy back to the fishmonger's where she skins mackerel every Saturday.

MELINDA: So you were thinking of the party's being tomorrow?

KATE: I asked Elsie, and she said she'd do anchovy-paste sandwiches and sausages on sticks stuck into a grapefruit and leave everything in the fridge. Me and the other girls can get the breakfast.

MELINDA: How many eggs?

KATE: Six would do. Most of us like water. Perhaps we should buy a Cornish pasty for Mr. Juniper, who's coming at eight in the morning to show me how to use the pedals on the harpsichord.

MELINDA: I could show you.

KATE: Yes, but Granddaddy says that when you get up at five in the morning to type, the secret things, God knows what they are—

MELINDA: Darling, it's rude to say "God" unless you go to church.

KATE: Everyone I know says it. Like "Parking." It doesn't mean what it sounds as if it meant.

MELINDA: What?

KATE: You know, a sign saying "Parking" when it means "No Parking."

MELINDA: I'd like to have got at least some of the flights of the staircase carpet cleaned before you had the party.

KATE: Nobody I know minds filth. Not ancient filth like ours.

## ACT III

*Six years later. For Gavin and Melinda, sitting at the same outdoor pub table, the passing of time is nothing. Renewed parasol. Same light sources, same view of the Georgian square, except that the mews houses behind the square are newly painted, with expensive cars parked in front of them. Orange trees and window boxes outside the little houses. The music is no longer organ music or singing from the church but disco music from the pub.*

GAVIN (*looking round for Kate*): To think it was always she who was saying "Everything's later." Now she's plain late.

MELINDA: She was impatient.

GAVIN: Still is.

MELINDA: She's got her own life to lead.

GAVIN (*gaily, bouncing up and down*): Shut up. What about us? Let's talk about us.

MELINDA: Leave her be.

GAVIN: She doesn't ask questions any longer.

MELINDA: She still likes the feeling of her hair down her back.

GAVIN: She washes it every day. The strands clog up the drainpipes. It's a very *long* house as well as a very *big* house. Thus, nearly a hundred feet of drainpipes clogged. I had a plumber in today and he said he had this long-hair trouble all over the square. He didn't mention which sex of hair. What's her job this week?

MELINDA: She's working in a Pakistani restaurant at night, and doing mime and learning Chinese in the daytime. The Chinese has been going on for months. She's been borrowing your Chinese books.

GAVIN: Yes, I noticed. Does she know she was born by a Caesarean?

MELINDA: Yes.

GAVIN: Does she really know her father won't see her?

MELINDA: Yes.

GAVIN: Twice untimely ripped. Once, more fondly.

MELINDA: Poor babe, and she's waited all this time until she's seventeen, and she's still not old enough to buy a drink in the pub.

GAVIN: Shall we give a party for her and open the claret we laid down for her when she was a girl and it couldn't be port?

MELINDA: The last party was all Coca-Cola, and somebody playing rock on the harpsichord let a candle drip into it. The whole top octave of the upper manual is dumb. Mr. Juniper the tuner is in despair.

GAVIN: Ring up *House & Garden*, or the emblem of good

housekeeping, or some column that gives household wrinkles.

MELINDA: I did. The nicest girl said I should iron the harpsichord with a warm iron through brown paper to absorb the wax. I tried to explain that you can't iron harpsichord strings and plectrums, but I don't think the girl quite understood the problem.

GAVIN: You don't say "girl" any longer, you say "woman," or "person." "Personhole cover."

MELINDA: What?

GAVIN: "Manhole cover." All the lost words will come back, though I daresay the women's-liberation hoo-ha will see us out. *(Looks round.)* Here comes the silent one. *(Kate emerges into the light of her old chair at the table.)*

GAVIN: What would you like to drink, darling?

KATE: Sorry I'm early.

GAVIN: You're not *early*. Where's your watch?

*(Kate shows him.)*

GAVIN: A Mickey Mouse watch?

KATE: It's Chinese. I don't mean Hong Kong.

GAVIN: What sort of time does it tell?

KATE: It may be Chinese time.

GAVIN: You mean it doesn't go?

KATE: It goes beautifully, but at its own pace.

MELINDA: Granddaddy was asking you what you wanted to drink. I'm afraid you're still not old enough to buy alcohol—

GAVIN:—though within an ace—

MELINDA:—but he'll get you some if you want it.

GAVIN: If I can stand going into that racket.

KATE: Could I have a Coke, please?

*(Gavin goes into the pub.)*

KATE: It's not a racket if you understand it.

MELINDA: No, I see that.

KATE: I thought I might go to China if I can learn enough Chinese first.

MELINDA: After Oxford? Mummy's worked rather hard

for that. I thought she looked a bit tired at dinner last night. Did you?

KATE: O.K., you don't want me to go to China. It's all very well for you. You've already been everywhere anyway. (*Pause*) Yes, Mummy did look a bit flaked, but she's fun.

MELINDA: You always did have pretty manners.

KATE: Is she lonely?

MELINDA: She's got a lot of friends. You'll see more of her as time goes by. She's still young.

KATE: Fairly.

MELINDA: One thing achieved.

KATE: And Daddy's new wife is very nice.

MELINDA: Yes. Which one?

KATE: The new one. My age. She's there when Daddy's asleep.

MELINDA: She's specially nice. The one he calls cheap to run.

KATE: It's a joke, but she doesn't like it much. He won't let her work, so that she can be made for him. And he gave her an old car for her birthday, so she can meet me at the station.

(*Gavin comes back with the drinks.*)

GAVIN: And some sausages, in case. Kate, we've got something serious to ask you. Would you rather have one of those mews cottages than the big house?

(*Kate is silent.*)

MELINDA: We were thinking that, with inflation, we'd be leaving you something much more valuable if we sold the big house and gave you one of the small ones.

GAVIN: The small ones have been so redecorated that they're worth more than the big ones, now that no one can splash out on maids and plumbing.

KATE: Granny, it's the house you've always had. Generations.

GAVIN: We don't want it to be a liability.

KATE: It's a present. You don't exchange presents. It's where you and Granddaddy got married from. When I was a little girl, you used to measure how much I'd grown on the big bathroom door and mark the places with the date. Everything's there. Granddaddy's library. The Chinese books. No.

*(Gavin walks away for a moment.)*

MELINDA: It's only a place.

*(Kate, in panic, calms herself by looking at Gavin's back.)*

KATE *(muttering)*: In trust. *(Pause)* Is he doing maths in his head the way he does in the morning when you're practicing the harpsichord?

MELINDA: I should imagine he's thinking. Often you have to keep your own counsel or else you get into very deep waters.

# We're Here

ON an old, unenlightened day, the undiscovered suddenly illuminated the prospect. An aged ex-judge, addressing his plate in an expensive restaurant, in a shout because he was deaf, said to a slightly younger woman who always heard him perfectly because she watched his lips: "Where's the gravy?"

The waiter hesitated, knowing him. The ex-judge's order of veal was covered in gravy.

"There's some on the plate, dear," said the woman. She had a hat on, because they were dining at half-past six, and the feathers in the hat bobbed gaily as she nodded toward the plate.

"Non-visible gravy. Trust it's palpable," he yelled.

"It is," said the old woman, taking a forkful. "Forgive me, I didn't mean to take that. We never liked eating off each other's plates."

There was a long pause. "Ann's got a bridge club going," said the woman.

"That's a *statement* you've just made. How do you *know?*"

"Ann told me."

The ex-judge waved the veal away. "That's hearsay." He asked for some soup. "Thick soup. Sieved," he shouted. "You don't understand gravy."

She translated some of this into French for the waiter.

123

"She runs the lessons after the rush-hour," the woman said. Still looking at his now empty plate, the ex-judge said, "You're making another statement."

"No, Ann said so."

"That's the meaning of hearsay."

"I'm sorry, dear. I thought it meant what one heard and didn't fully understand. As I often do. You're used to pricking up your ears, in your profession."

"Impotent passions, early infirmities."

"Don't say that about yourself." Pause.

"I'm enjoying my delicious liver."

"Never could bring myself to get my teeth round offal, even as a small boy with a digestion like a diesel."

"I came round eventually to liver," she said softly, in the voice that he always heard.

His soup was brought. There was hubbub about new napkins.

"*Last* but not *least* to my *wife*, who *helped* in comp*i*ling the *in-dex*. The perfect hexameter," he said, tucking the napkin into the chain of his fob watch. "You don't mind about the wife? I thought of it in the night."

"It's very good."

"The napkin?"

"Very practical."

"And about the wife? Is the wife also all right?"

"Well, anything else would spoil the rhyme scheme."

"In any case she's tucked away with her horses in Gloucestershire," he said.

"You have really decided it's better she and I don't meet? I mean, it's been a long time."

"She knows about you. You know about her. What's the point? Of course, it might lead to some highjinks," shouted the ex-judge.

"Best left as it is," said the old woman, the feathers in her hat bobbing.

"We haven't got much time," yelled the ex-judge, who hadn't yet looked at her, and a waiter hurried up.

"The trolley, sir?" said the waiter.

"No!" shouted the ex-judge. "No one understands these days. No time for nonsense. I've just perfected my speed-reading." A young man at the next table turned on a transistor radio for the news. He got the weather.

"What's he saying?" shouted the ex-judge.

The old woman said softly "It's a wireless, dear. It's the weather." She repeated the forecast to him sentence by sentence.

"That's what makes me laugh," said the ex-judge. "They give you a day-to-day idea of the weatehr but they can't give you a long-range forecast."

"Who can, darling?" said the old woman.

"If thought is life, and strength, and breath, / And the want of thought is death—" he said.

"Then am I a happy fly, / If I live, or if I die," she said back.

He looked at her for the first time and noticed laugh-lines round her mouth. "You're a young woman, you know. You shouldn't be spending your time with an old codger like me."

"My birthday's after yours."

"But you've kept yourself fit. Lovely figure. Gibson Girl figure," he barked, and she blushed, because people were looking. His voice was something that she was used to alone with him, but in the company of others she heard him through their ears.

Waiters passed. "Raspberries!" he said loudly. The waiters were Greek and merely smiled. "Raspberries!!" he said more loudly still. "This place has gone to pot."

"You're being difficult. They'll come."

"When you think of the world, give it one more lash from me."

"Don't cultivate dudgeon, dear."

The raspberries came. The ex-judge complained of the seeds and ate only the whipped cream. "What?" he kept saying.

"Let's not make any dates early this week. It's a festive time," said the old woman, taking his eye to make sure he could hear.

"Let's play it by ear," said the ex-judge.

The old woman piled more whipped cream onto the ex-judge's plate.

"Blasted seeds," he said. "Get stuck in your teeth. I've still got all the teeth that I was born with."

"That you were at Winchester with."

"Manner of speaking."

"Yes. Oh, Penny went to a funeral last week. Very very young man, not more than thirty-three. He'd never been off his feet and he went to bed and didn't get up again. Never had a thing wrong with him." She finished her raspberries. "As far as he knew."

"I sometimes feel a sense of peace and I realize it's because I'm not talking," he shouted. "What was that about Ann and bridge?"

"She's giving bridge lessons."

"Where?"

"Five days a week, five evenings, in her hotel."

"You never cared for bridge."

"You never had time for it and by then I had to go home."

"Home!" yelled the ex-judge. "A hostile witness would call it a rooming house."

"Well, we're getting on."

"On to what? I have dreams of squash. I was always nimble on my feet."

"Still are," she said fondly.

"I want a bill," he said to a passing waiter. "And we'll have a shandy while we're waiting. One shandy, two glasses."

"Everything all right, sir?" said the headwaiter kindly.

"A bill," said the ex-judge, not wasting words.

"Testy old bird," said the young man next door with the transistor.

"She's lighting a cigarette, see? That woman over there," shouted the ex-judge to the old woman, looking across the room at another guest.

The woman across the dining room, who was eighty-eight and as deaf as he was except when she wanted to hear, yelled, "And why shouldn't I?" puffing at her cigarette.

"Quite right too. She's well within her rights. It's certainly not cocaine," shouted the ex-judge confidentially.

He drummed his fingers.

"Heard something on the BBC. It interests me very much, the likeness between Gaelic and Spanish. Heard an announcer remarking on it yesterday before you'd have been up. Said he couldn't find the word in Gaelic for *mañana*. Scotsman said there was such a word in Gaelic but it didn't imply the same degree of urgency. The idea interests me very much." He stuck out his foot at a passing waiter and said, with no more or less impatience than before, "I want a bill." The bill came. "You check it," he said to the old woman. "How much for the drink?"

"One pound twenty-five."

"Each?"

"Together."

"Should have said. Waiters are getting sloppy." He paid the bill in beautiful clean crisp notes and gave the old woman three pounds for tips. "You get out first. Ah. Before you go, they tell me the people in my hotel are getting younger."

The couple next door had assumed they were married.

"Students?" said the old woman, looking pretty and revived by his readiness to move.

"Not students. People." He put his hands on the table, and said, "Don't give the man the tip until he's pulled the table out." His friend got out herself, and he said, "You were always slender."

There was a delay. No one came to help him. Spectators in

the restaurant took the crusty old man to be obstinate. The old woman walked quickly to the front doors and then slowly back to the table and looked at him covertly. He heaved himself to his feet by his own efforts. A great bulk, bent nearly double, though he had seemed slim and upright when he was sitting at the table. His chauffeur came eventually, after the ex-judge had struggled along adjoining tables, his weight mostly on his knuckles, and lifted him on to his shoulders. Not a sack. A vivid man. His friend held his hand as he was carried out. "Get some raspberries without pips for us next time," he said to the headwaiter.

"The usual table? Would it be easier nearer the door?"

"I like to be at the far end. My friend feels the drafts."

# Twice Lucky

A SHIP'S steward came round a nearly deserted boat deck in a gale with a tray of bouillon. A girl named Eliza and a young painter named Rawley took a mug each and clasped their hands round them for warmth, sitting in deck chairs under rugs. Rawley looked at the Atlantic in silence for a long time. Eliza also looked, searching for what he saw in it.

"You have beautiful hair," Rawley said, without turning round.

"It's a disappointment to my niece."

"You're too young to have a niece."

"I'm twenty-four."

"Still too young,"

"She's four. My sister's two years older than I am."

Rawley didn't move his eyes from the ocean. He emitted grief. "I'm going to be thirty on this voyage," he said, as if bracing himself to the admission of a sorry private loss.

Eliza thought the melancholy was a joke, but then realized that the birthday was going to be a hard day for him to get through. Pause.

Rawley rallied. "Why was your hair a disappointment to your niece?"

"My sister had told her it was red when the little girl hadn't met me. She'd been looking forward to it. I lived in Ohio and

129

they were in Maine. She was very good for twenty minutes when we did meet, and then she burst into tears because she said my hair wasn't red like her toy telephone. She said it was brown like her desk. Of course, she was quite right. Red hair is really wood-colored."

Rawley turned round at last and looked at her carefully. "I should say it was red, myself."

"But then you paint that way."

"What do you mean?"

"As if you had very thin eyelids."

"Perhaps they'll thicken as I get older." Gloom. "Even on this voyage, I expect. I'll be thirty by the time we dock. No one over thirty has thin eyelids. They thicken, like souls."

Eliza paused. "Souls don't thicken with age. Not necessarily."

"Not in the case of yours."

"I didn't mean anything bad about your paintings."

"Of course you did. You meant they were feverish, obviously," said Rawley.

"I'm saving up for one. I think they're calm."

"Could I paint you?"

She paused, and wished she knew him well enough to do something other than smile and nod. "Thank you," she said.

"We'll do it tomorrow."

"What are you thinking about?"

"About the judge in Washington who put two clerks of the court in jail for a week because they lost a file. There was no need for him to go bonkers," said Rawley.

"Judges are supposed to be capable of systematic doubt."

"You sound like a surgeon. Did you do philosophy?"

"No. I worked after high school. But I hadn't enough to do, and I read books out of my bottom office drawer where the towel and soap dish were."

Another twenty minutes went by. Rawley continued to look at her. He wondered if he were going to fall in love with her. She was extremely paintable. He painted her in his head, and also painted the sea. "I'm painting the sea," he said. "I paint by ear. My eyes really are very bad. I'm afraid I'm likely to be blind quite soon. I can't see at all when I get up."

"I've got some eyedrops."

"If I'm going to stop being able to see I'd better think instead."

Eliza guessed that he was again drably contemplating being thirty. "Thirty really isn't very old," she said.

"Fatal if one were a rock musician, and far from good if one were a mathematician. Do you suppose I shall have time to prepare myself for another profession by the time we dock?"

"You could be a writer from the sound of it."

"The characteristics of capitalism readying itself for combat are no background for a writer. Fear, opportunism, violence, seediness. An ebb of things."

"That's not what you paint."

"What do I paint?" he said, looking at the sea, thinking of his canvases of the U.S. stamp.

"Value?" Eliza said, after a pause, also thinking of the canvases of the U.S. stamp.

"That was difficult to say?"

"You're not really concerned about your eyes. It's your *birthday* that's on your mind, isn't it?"

"You're grinning," he said, looking at the sea, and then grinning himself because he had just seen a pair of tights high above them supported in midair by a blast of steam from a funnel.

She followed his eyes. "People say I paint peculiar things," he said.

"I don't say that." The tights looked both drab and mad.

A seaman came down from a ladder braced against the funnel, from which he had been just unable to reach the tights, and asked if either of them had a steel coat hanger that he could use for reaching.

"Not on me," said Eliza.

"Down in my cabin," said Rawley.

Eliza knotted a rope round a weight, climbed the ladder, swung the rope round her head and trapped the fluttering tights. Rawley held the ladder and admired her. The seaman, flustered, disappeared to ask the purser whether the ship's company was insured if a passenger should hurt himself hooking tights.

"The tights haven't even got a hole in them," said Eliza. "Is the sailor humiliated?"

"He's gone to ask the purser whether the company's insured."

"What were you thinking of while I was up there?"

"Why do you always ask that?"

"I don't know you, so I can't guess."

"Yet," said Rawley.

"The end of the trip's only five days away," Eliza said. "But you'll be over the hurdle of thirty by the time we're done."

She has a soft heart with a cutting edge, Rawley thought. He momentarily bled within. "Oh Lord," he said. "Where are we now? What's that land?"

"Not even Wales yet. Ireland, I think."

Rawley fumed and felt hungry. "Wales has contributed nothing but a whine to the history of European civilization."

Eliza had already learned to distinguish his real indignation from his jabs. She said nothing. He thanked her silently.

"Could we have lunch together?" he said.

"With grandfather and his nursing sister?" said Eliza, firmly, looking at an old man sitting at the other end of the deck. "The nurse is in her cabin. They're going to a conference together in England. She knows his ways."

"Is that your grandfather, then?"

"Yes. I promised about lunch." She waved at the old man, who had taken them both in.

Rawley looked in the old man's direction, met his eyes, shivered. "I'm ravenous."

"It's because you've been painting in your head."

"It's because I've been doing nothing." She held his hand and he softened. "I wish I *had* been painting," he said. "I feel like a corpse. Heavy but empty. Why are dead weights heavy? They say it has something to do with inertia. The body no longer managing."

"RAWLEY," she said, quite a while later, "thirty isn't really *very* old."

"You're lonely, aren't you?"

She sat silently, and caught a bird feather blown in the wind.

"And now you're angry with me," he said.

"This is no time to surrender to feelings of hostility and pique. Historically speaking."

"It's English people who always speak historically," he said. "Americans like us have an instinct to break things up and start again."

She looked about to cry. "Don't you break this up, whatever it is. Not for a few days. Being English by birth, I'm allowed to speak historically."

"*Are* you English by birth? I thought you said you came from Ohio."

"No. I only live there."

"Since when?"

"Since I was three."

"English people stay English forever. Nothing to be done. But your grandfather's American, at least."

"Yes."

"You're an orphan."

"Yes."

"It was your father who was English?"

"Yes."

THE PHYSICIAN, named Logan Decker, was seventy-nine. His London-born nursing sister, named Amelia Mortimer, aged forty-nine, was below deck feeling seasick. Dr. Decker went down to her cabin and asked her to marry him. She groaned with illness, smiled at him, said "Yes," and tried to take his pulse. The doctor grasped her hand. His hands shook, as usual, though they never shook when he was reading medical literature.

"Eliza says that Rawley Pound is on board," said the doctor.

"Who's he?"

"The famous painter. He paints the stamp. Of various costs. We're obviously going to have lunch with them both. You could have some clear soup, if you're up to it?"

"Clear soup is all that sea-travel is. They bring it to one for elevenses and then they offer it to one for lunch. And all the while you're paying a packet for me, dear. For smoked salmon and I don't know what." She was sick at the thought. When she came back from the bathroom, the doctor produced a ring from his old-fashioned watch pocket.

"But I've seen you wearing it, the amethyst, beautiful, as a weight for your fob watch," said Amelia. "What'll you do without it?"

"I always thought it would suit you."

"It's re-set."

"I had it done in Washington."

"How did you know I'd say yes?"

"I hoped you might." He sat down on her bed. "After all this time, I mean. Did I wait too long?"

She kissed his hand. She smelled of an expensive scent. "It's 'Joy,'" she said. "The advertisements say, 'The costliest perfume in the world.'"

She knelt up on the bed to look out of the porthole. "I thought the Atlantic was supposed to be as calm as glass in autumn. It looks more like corrugated iron to me." She collapsed again, and kissed his hand again. "Look at me. A wreck. When I should be taking care of you. Look at *us*. Getting *engaged*, and me laid up. What was Eliza's young man's name?"

"Rawley Pound."

"He sounds more English than American, Dr. Decker. Is she safe with him? The English are very romantic at sea."

"He's the most American painter we have. You can't go on calling me Dr. Decker in private, and from now on everything's going to be in private. Everything possible. Think of it! No more appointments! No more white overalls! No more blunders about my instruments when you've forgotten!"

"You're the grumpiest man I ever worked for."

"One patient lately said I was a *great* man," said the doctor with dignity.

"Grumpiness and greatness have been known to go together. I daresay I get the grumpy side more after working with you for nearly thirty years."

"Plenty of girls applied at the time. but I picked you because I liked your spunk and I liked your elbows."

"*Elbows?*"

"When you rolled up your sleeves to scrub up. Of course, knees didn't show then. It was the New Look."

"Elbows?" She drew away. "Is that all?"

"No, not nearly all."

She saw he wasn't going to go on. He was never one to respond to prodding. "This painter. Is he one in a garret?"

"I said he was famous. His paintings of stamps, American stamps, sell for thousands of dollars. Thousands and thousands."

"Well, now, isn't that nice?" Then she paused. "Is it, though? I thought you didn't like emblems." She went into the bathroom and felt poorly again. The doctor shouted politely through the bathroom door after a while. "I don't think he does, either," he said. "He's more interested in white serrated edges and straight lines of hard-edged color. As shapes."

"Why not circles?" said Amelia through the locked door, running a bath. "Why not the bars of the Union Jack, come to that? If he's so interested in shapes?

"The Union Jack, now: that's an unusual shape. Stripes. Stripes with *very* hard edges. A lot of people don't notice the disparity in the width of the stripes and they hang the flag upside down, but a painter wouldn't make that mistake. Will you hand me my dressing gown through the door, sir?"

He was so used by now to being called "sir" by her that he forgot for the moment about getting her in the habit of using his Christian name, merely handing her the dressing gown through the door.

"You can wear the ring in the bath," he said. "It's quite safe. I had the stone cemented into the setting because you've always got your hands in water. There's no need to get married if you don't want to. Engaged is quite enough if you'd prefer it, though marriage would enable me to provide for you better after my death."

"You're as right as rain," said Amelia, running the taps more fiercely.

"I'm seventy-nine. Still, provided the world doesn't blow itself up in the next fifty years, disaster probably won't reach the well-off like us."

"We're not well-off. You overpay me. Of course, now that we're engaged you can forget about wages."

"You'll get the same as before," the doctor said firmly, and paused.

Amelia shouted through the door, "Are you all right?"

"I was thinking what a pretty color your dressing gown is."

"Yellow?"

"Summery."

"Eliza's painter wouldn't care for it if he's stuck on stamp colors. Is he worth her, sir?"

He remembered to correct her this time, and shouted, "You'd better call me Logan, as I said. If it comes to my being an invalid in need of respect we can think again, but by then I should suppose we'll be in the habit. Shall you like seeing England after all this time? Come up on deck, dear. You'll feel better. And then we'll lunch with Eliza and the painter. You will come up, won't you?"

"You say he's famous. I'm not mixing with the hoi-de-polloi."

"I'm fairly famous, and you don't seem to mind me," said Logan.

"The professions are different." She came out of the bathroom with her hair down.

"You look about seventeen," Logan said.

Amelia hid behind a wardrobe door to get dressed in a white suit with a sailor tie that she had bought for the voyage. Every now and again she stretched out a hand to the wall to steady herself because of the rocking of the boat. "I'm forty-nine," she said.

"But wiry," he said.

"Like you," she said.

"You realize we've already seen a century out, between us?" he said. "There's every chance we'll reach the year 2050, jointly, provided the food holds out. It's like the oil supply. People don't seem to realize how short it is."

Amelia suddenly looked suspicious. "And what does this famous painter paint his stamps in? Water color?"

"Oil," said Logan.

"There you are," said Amelia. "He's a smart-aleck. He doesn't pay heed to the supplies you're worrying your busy head about."

"The amount of oil he uses on a canvas in infinitesimal, even when he paints big. It wouldn't drive a Fiat two yards. It wouldn't heat your clear soup, my dove. May I use your looking glass?"

"I remember how impressed I was when I first came to you by the way you didn't say 'mirror.'"

"I'm very old, you know. Old American is much like English. I wouldn't say 'dig,' or 'smart' for 'clever,' for example. Or 'neat,' in the new sense. Every five-year-old seems to say 'neat' now and I don't quite take their meaning."

"You make too much of your age, my dear." She took his blood pressure. "Your heart's like a boy's. Same as a girlfriend's of mine in England. Mrs. Ransome. She's passed away now but when I knew her she'd never had a day's illness in her life and she was eighty-four. She would often go out with nothing on but a little suit. She went around with eighteen pounds in her bag from her pension for months and I said, 'Dear, you've got to put it in the post office savings. You can't go around carrying eighteen pounds.' But she wouldn't do it. She lived upstairs. She was a bit ga-ga but very trim. She'd look at me and say. 'Who are you?' I'd known her for twelve years. She'd say, 'I don't know who you are,' or 'You live upstairs.' 'Downstairs,' I'd say. 'So you're the lady from upstairs,' she'd say, stubborn. 'Downstairs, dear,' I'd say. 'I keep telling you.' She wouldn't hear anything about the eighteen pounds and it worried me. How does my sailor tie look? Oh, this boat."

"We're running alongside a storm."

"I said to the vicar, can you come in and talk to Mrs. Ransome? The vicar was a good man. He'd got a respect for her. She used to work for the elderly when she was young. We're all going to be old one day. Forgetful. Then she married a man forty years older than herself so she stopped her job, though she was carrying on the work in a way in her private life, I suppose. The vicar spent two hours with her before she let him near her handbag. He came downstairs with the eighteen pounds eventually and put it in the post office for her and gave me the book to prove it. My husband had reached the point where he'd go mad if he saw her."

"You're *married?*" Logan stared at his ring on her finger, stricken.

"I was only seventeen. He ran off with a probationary nurse in a year. That's what made me go in for nursing. I daresay. That, and of course the necessity of keeping myself."

"It would be bigamy if you're married," shouted the doctor, as if she had muddled up his appointments.

"I've got a divorce, dear. Don't shout. I've got the decree in my luggage with my papers. I'm afraid it cost him a bit but he wanted to marry the girl."

"So then you came to America."

"Yes. To go on about Mrs. Ransome: as I say, my husband had reached breaking point. She'd always be dropping in to listen to the radio with us and explain it. My husband would start yelling that he knew perfectly well what the BBC was saying, thank you very much. To shut her up. Or he'd go out for a glass of water."

"You never told me all this."

"Or maybe he was going out to see his wife-to-be, looking back on things. I never thought of that before, you know. So what I began to do with Mrs. Ransome was just pop in when I knew she was in bed and say, 'It's only me, dear.' One day her face was as black as a coal-sweep's. 'Let me give you a wash, dear,' I said. 'I wash twice a day,' she said. But she was filthy, all the same. All over her cheeks. I know what she must have done. She'd been reading the newspaper and she must have covered her face with newsprint by holding her hands up to it to think. She was as thin as a sparrow, I remember, but between retreats to bed, which weren't in the cause of invalidism but more like sprees in her head, she gave tremendous tea parties with ladyfingers and layer cake. She didn't lack for friends in spite of the bouts of rest. She took them out on the eighteen pounds from the post office for the last do before I left to work for you. She made me get the vicar. 'Vicar,' she said, 'I can't find my handbag and I need my eighteen pounds. Amelia gave me the receipt last Christmas and the receipt is in my handbag but I can't find it, as I say. I expect it's been thieved.' 'It'll be under the pillow, dear,' I said. 'I've looked under the pillow,' she said. But there it was. So the vicar went to the post office and got out the eighteen pounds, and she did this slap-up tea with gentlemen's relish and buttered crumpets in spite of butter being so dear, and everyone came. Then she was very quiet for two days and I went round to the vicar and said, 'We'd best have a doctor.' We got my lady doctor. I remember how beautifully spoken she always was. She came with the vicar to be introduced, but Mrs. Ransome said, 'I don't mix with doctors,' and closed the door on them after they'd had a spot of what was left of the gentlemen's relish sandwiches. Life wasn't too good to her after that but I heard she was soon up and about again like in the old days, going out to baby-sit and prepare tea parties. A friend wrote to me and told me. The pension officials were kind to her, she said. She didn't let on about her earnings, because the government would have cut her pension. Though I daresay she meant the officials turned a blind eye."

He watched her get up. He stood for her and said, "If one can't immediately change history, which physicians can't, let alone pension officers, one can at least serve people who are prone to it."

Amelia looked at him and said. "That's what I'd expect you to say. That's what you do, I've often thought. Is this painter good enough for Eliza, then? To be your grandson-in-law?"

BOTH couples were now on deck, many yards distant.

"I've just realized it's the Sunday nearest to November the eleventh," said Amelia.

"What's November the eleventh, dear?"

"Armistice Day. Poppy Day. It's nearly eleven o'clock in England and we have a two-minute silence at eleven o'clock. All the traffic stops. All the tractors."

She had a shortwave radio with her that she held to her ear with the transmitting receiver rising from her head like an antenna. "I can't find London. It is eleven, isn't it? I wish they'd turn off that Tannoy. It's like Muzak."

"It is Muzak."

She got a rock group on the radio. "That's Pink Floyd," said Logan. "That must be England."

"No, there'd be silence."

"How can you find a silence on a radio?"

She tuned into a station where there was suddenly the sound of a cannon. She stood up and looked at the ocean. Logan took off his hat but remained seated. Eliza heard the cannon, looked at the date on her ship's newspaper and shook her head in the effort to remember something. Two minutes later there were more cannon. Amelia sat down again.

"That was Hyde Park Corner," she said. "The cannon go off in Hyde Park. You shouldn't have taken off your hat in this cold. Bitter. I thought I saw your granddaughter trying to recall something. Would it be England?"

"She only thinks of it sometimes."

"What a strange topic for a young American painter, now, the national stamp."

"I daresay it's a jest that interests him technically."

"People who make the public admire them for their wit must fear for their memory."

She was always surprising, thought Logan. She interests, that's the thing, even if she is a dreadful nurse when she gets near an appointment book. People are her forte.

They had lunch together, the four of them. Nobody had any dinner. They were running into the eye of the storm now. Logan came and sat with Amelia in her cabin for a while and refilled her hot-water bottle. Rawley asked Eliza if he could come to her cabin. Feeling cheerful and in love, though sleepy with hunger, she said yes.

She went to sleep before she meant to, leaving her light still burning. Rawley started to draw her. She looked beautiful, but the sketch was academic. He tore up the drawing, half-meaning to wake her for the sake of the comfort of talking to her, but she slept on, with her hair over one of her pillows like a child's.

Rawley crept out and set up a 16mm camera, meaning to make an eight-hour film of her asleep. Small movements. The little death. Reconciliation with time's passage.

He stood by the camera, watching, in love with her, hoping now that she wouldn't wake, and not for the sake of his film. Dreams made her stir. She said something in her sleep. "The man who loses his dreams is lost." An aboriginal saying.

At 3 A.M. the rocking of the boat jerked Eliza against the wall and then back against a pillow that was lying down the length of the bed. "I'm sorry," she said in her sleep. "I thought you were someone I knew"; legs thrashing, and then stopping as if she were in a crowded street and had been running after a man she thought she recognized.

3:20 A.M. "Rawley," she said in her sleep, "It's time to get up." "No, it isn't, Eliza," Rawley said into her ear, tucking the blankets more tightly around her. She sighed heavily.

3:30 A.M. "Where are you?" she said in her sleep.

5:00 A.M. Three loud bumps from somewhere. Cases falling? Like cannon.

She held her forehead in recapture and then started to get out of the sheets. Rawley understood the buried recall that the sounds had dug up, and helped the somnambulist with the bedclothes.

In her sleep, she stood by the bed, taking off a polo-neck sweater of his that he had given her for warmth, and then positioning herself to attention naked, like an old soldier with his hat doffed. Rawley let the film go on running and started to draw her again.

# One Asks Oneself

DEAR Peter, the Hon. Peter Duncan Borthwick, my first cousin, is a small, thin man packed with interest for anyone who can be troubled to listen to him through his silences. The silences at his house, Clayes, in Gloucestershire, have been very long, but they are worth putting up with, as Peter is worth putting up with. As, indeed, the whole taciturn family has been so long worth putting up with. He inherited Clayes, which is colossal, when his elder brother was killed in the Second World War. He nominally inherited the peerage, too, but formally declined it on the ground that he was a member of the House of Commons and wanted to go on being one, although he has since twice resigned on matters of principle and has had to wait in the cold until a new Government came around to his view. A new Tory Government. He votes the opposing way from me, but he has always listened to the Labour Opposition, as to others.

As to this matter of listening: well, Peter pays heed, you see. During those long silences at Clayes when he is putting his napkin back into his silver napkin ring. Or the silences that seemed even longer, when we were both eighteen and he would take me out to have dinner and would spend half an hour between forkfuls of grouse, bread sauce, fried bread, Brussels sprouts, and game chips, raising the forkful to his mouth and then, after a little talk, lowering it again, dampening one's hopes of progress toward bed—as I say, during those silences there is much of interest. When we were eighteen there was even a flicker of eroticism between us. We knew it was forbidden, because of our being first cousins, but it was there. He would talk to me between the delayed forkfuls, having put down the knife and fork to move his wrists in a rowing motion: feathering imaginary oars as they came out of the water. At Eton, being small, he had been the cox of the boat, and I followed the University boat in the official launch three years running at the Oxford and Cambridge boat race. He wasn't rowing himself, of course, being a cox, but the feathering had told me that he would have loved it. There are probably many other things he would love to do.

Let me try to describe him. He never will, though he writes a good deal on topics of the moment and of history. When he chooses to publish, what he has to say is taken with sobriety and concern, but he never writes about himself. I think he would regard that as near to writing fiction. Fiction is something he would love to dare but won't. Ever, I'm sure. I believe he would think of it as some sort of intrusion by an interloper unequipped. He is never intrusive. Other people's skills are their tended land. He would hate himself if he poached.

And so, to draw a deep breath. As to his looks: he is about six foot, thin, ravenous for starch and sugar. I once, quite lately, put a bar of milk chocolate on his pillow. He came into my room and said, "Provisions for going up Everest," and went out again: to read Surtees, I should think—perhaps "Mr. Sponge's Sporting Tour," his favorite—or a history of the Peninsular War. His life has often been a matter of going up Everest. His shoulders slope downward, like a jug. He has our family's deep-brown eyes. In the way of portraiture, there is something about his face—always has been—that is prescient, an augury of what it is going to look like at eighty.

Though I know him to be convival beyond the reach of most, and so funny that he has often made me gasp for breath as if I were drowning, there is a sternness in his face. The sternness is exerted against himself. When he feels especially disciplinary, he goes for a walk with his dog (or me, which is less anodyne). We are very fond of each other. Whenever I am staying at Clayes he draws a bath for me, with beautiful scent in it from Trumper, in Curzon Street, and it is difficult for both of us not to share the bath. Because of the past, you see. He finds the present hard to dwell in.

As to Clayes: I must have spent almost as many school holidays there as Peter did. It is sixteenth century and huge, with a matchless library. His first wife was one of a set of famous beautiful American sisters. She was as tall as he, and almost speechless. Bossy, I thought. The staff didn't take to her. She wanted non-coffee coffee, and monogrammed note-pads at Christmas saying "Take to London" in dark brown on pale brown and "Take to country" in pale brown on dark brown. She wanted to be in London, I think, where Peter had a one-room pied-à-terre. She suddenly went to London to have their babies—boy twins—although she had been going for eight and a half months to a perfectly good Gloucestershire gynecologist. She said out of the blue, while she was doing petit point, that she was lonely for the sight of a Hilton. So Peter of course went with her to London, though not, preserve us, to a Hilton, and they sat it out in his single room. She went at ten one night into a nursing home to have the twins, and Peter was told to come back at nine the next morning. After little sleep he set off at seven from the flat, walking the three miles to the nursing home to spin out the waiting time, and the doctor met him on the doorstep and said that she didn't want to see him.

"I'm lonely for New York," she said to me at Clayes a few weeks later.

Peter came in and heard. He hears almost everything. He looked concussed. "Oh, sweetheart, always ask for help," he

said, holding her, but she turned away. When she left him
and England, she took with her a good deal of alimony, but
later on, with tacit goodness, she sent it back. She left her
babies. Her time in England must have cost her toll. She
found the life chilly, I know, and her family-by-marriage
bookish in a way that extended to her no companionship. If
she had been older, perhaps. If, if. And in the meantime the
twins. Peter found a Scottish nanny called Diana Ross to look
after them. Clayes has a gallery on the bedroom floor, circling
the double staircase; I remember that I was once staying there
when the twins were five, and that I was looking for an empty
loo, and that any of the beautiful wooden doors off the gallery
seemd to open in turn onto the sight of an identical sailor-
suited little boy nearly swallowed up by the antique depths of
a mahogany loo with a chain too high for him to reach. Each
looked cold and sad.

"Shall we play Patience?" I said when I had found the first.
"Shall we play Double Patience?" I said to the second. "All
together, starting in thirty seconds, in my room, because of
the fur rug, for warmth, and the gramophone? Double
Patience goes very fast and it also goes very well to Scarlatti."

They were adorable. Are. They are now eleven. Diana,
being Scots, is classless; and Diana, being Diana, is a learner.
She has become their tutor. She has taught herself Latin and
Greek. She is not possessive.

WE are a silent family. Our houses and flats and luggage,
wherever we travel, sag with books. I go abroad a lot, always
only with hand luggage, but from the weight of the bag no
one can ever believe that they hold hardly anything but books
and notebooks. Duty-free booze, people think. Heavily
wrapped bombs done up in mauve fake-satin bows.

Peter's and my grandmother, the dowager duchess, wears
one of two beautifully dry-cleaned couture suits all the year
round. She is not someone to pay notice to hem lengths, but
she pays a deal of notice to talk. She is tentative and deaf. She

rates herself low. Her arthritis is bad. She is ninety-three. She comes often to Clayes, and we spoke about it in London over sherry, very loudly.

"I went up last Friday-to-Monday to Clayes. Lovely time. Peter does like all his trees, doesn't he?" she said, pouring me a large dollop of the very best sherry, and herself a mixture of sweet Cinzano and Lillet. "Now, what's this in the Middle East?"

I stayed standing, naturally, until she was in her chair. The *Radio Times*, the *Guardian*, the *Times*, the *Telegraph*, the *Financial Times*, the *Wall Street Journal*, the *International Herald Tribune*, the London junk papers were beside her on one little Chippendale table. The current Hansard of Parliamentary goings-on and a pile of White Papers and Blue Books were on another, with a pencil sharpened by her maid, and her lorgnette.

"Clayes is too big," I said.

"That's what I think. Gold going up, everything going up, have to draw in our belts. On the other hand, he does love it. Peter. He thinks there, don't you see."

"So do the twins."

"But they'll be thinking soon at school, darling."

"And there's Diana, and Annabel."

"Annabel?"

"They're going to get married."

"I thought they already would be. Tell me, what does she do, darling? Does she work and things, like you? I'm so interested." She patted the pile of Government papers and then leaned forward to cup her hand over her ear. "What was that?"

"Annabel writes about cooking and kitchen gadgets."

"Nice girl, is she?"

"Very."

"That was my impression. Good to Peter, I thought. Understood about Clayes. That poor American beauty never did, did she? Very cold, she found it. I think she expected there'd be lots of hunt balls. If it hadn't been for Peter, of course, I daresay there might have been, but hunt balls aren't of much interest, are they? There's a painting of Giorgione's with everybody strewn about that always makes one think of hunt balls. Awfully exhausting and barren, don't you think?"

We talked more about Annabel.

"Kitchen gadgets," said my grandmother. "By Jove. Does she get published?"

"Oh, yes. Every Sunday."

"I expect she makes a packet, People do, promoting clothes and things. Poor Peter is rather badly off, but aren't we all?"

"Why is he a Tory, Gram?"

"Well, we all are, aren't we? Except you. It runs in the family. Now, we've got lamb cutlets, and they're beckoning. How do you feel toward a lamb cutlet, darling? You don't eat enough."

We went along to her dining room and had potted shrimps, lamb cutlets with mashed potatoes and peas, and cheese.

"And did you go to China?" said Gram, eating very little.

I told her about it, speaking even more loudly than was needed, in a way that upset her maid, who remembered her more clearly from the times when her mistress could hear.

"And so what do you make of Communism, eh?" said Gram, three of whose closest relations had been in Tory Cabinets.

I talked to her at length—probably redundantly, I thought—about Yugoslavian Communism, and then at even greater length about Cuba. She knew in detail about Yugoslavia. Cuba she didn't respond to, but she listened carefully. Twenty minutes later, questions followed scraps of information I had given her about Cuba's literacy programs. She kept on nodding sympathetically. In the end, talk was stopped, because she said, "So you think she is a worthwhile woman?" and it became clear that she had heard only the *a* ending on *Cuba* and taken the island to be a person.

\*    \*    \*

PETER'S beloved Clayes was indeed too big. Our grandmother's parting words to me, she clutching Hansard, had
been "Darling, we must draw in our horns." Clayes, which
had seen many a change in its time—Roman Catholic to
Church of England, medieval to Romantic, Gothic to
Gothick, an eighteenth-century wing and terrace added to its
sixteenth-century beginnings—was actually in the midst of
being made smaller. The minimization was going to cost my
decent cousin nearly a million pounds. Houses-as-metaphors-
of-England's-economy department. Hell's bells. Our family
doesn't go in for metaphors much. It's simply that Peter was
having this rebuilding done, without melancholy, and that in
the meantime he was living with his new wife, Annabel, and
his two sons and his butler, Crewe, in Crewe's cottage, which
was the North Lodge. Peter being Peter, he was of course
paying Crewe rent and constantly apologizing for intrusion.

We were having dinner: Crewe in his butler's clothes,
embarrassed to be sharing his minute house; Peter looking
gaunt, though well bestowed by Annabel; the twins vanish-
ing up to bed; Annabel, wearing a caftan, being comic and
reposeful. She has blue eyes that are the color of del-
phiniums. Freckled skin. An upturned nose. She was press-
ing down on it as if she hated it.

"Annabel, what are you doing?" said Peter.

"Trying to cure my nose. It's a clown's nose."

"Don't meddle with it. I like it." He waited, and took some
scrambled egg and smoked trout from Crewe. "Thank you."
He gave himself very little, being thin, and getting thinner. I
could see Crewe looking at him, worried, and when he came
round to my place he said as much, but all I could find to say
back to him quickly was "You know him. Don't fret. It's the
house being changed, and so on."

Annabel was being merry at her end of the cramped table
and singing "Addio, addio," from Così Fan Tutte.

"Annabel made the sauce with a gadget called Cuisinart
that costs heaven knows what. Isn't it good? She got the

gadget for very little because of writing about it."

Crewe said, "It's French, sir. It wouldn't cost so much if we hadn't gone into the bloody Common Market, sir. Bleeding Frogs. I beg your pardon, knowing your feelings about French Lit."

"Well, Proust was one thing but Napoleon another, and all those French housewives now are more Napoleonic than Proustian, coming over here on the ferry because of the exchange being in their favor, and poking our meat as if Soho were their *boucherie*."

"For all that, you still get the twins to learn French beautifully, and you still keep rereading Balzac," said Annabel. "And you talk about the fall of Paris as if it were the end of heroism."

Crewe said, "I think he hates Pétain, Madam, you see. We can't forget Vichy at our age."

I looked at him to get him to shut up, and he nodded.

Crewe handed round a crème brûlée. When asked, he talked with pride about the way he had scorched it at the finish, in a tray of iced water under the grill. He had one hand behind his back as he was handing the dish round. "Sir," he said, "the builders tell me they have shrunk the ballroom successfully by forty feet lengthwise and forty feet widthwise. Now they are studying the lowering of the ceiling. It will mean new piping, sir."

"Estimates."

"The new piping will cost a tidy bit."

"Yes."

"I suppose it will save on the oil in the end. But to think that you resigned over Suez, sir."

"The right thing to do, I believe. At the time."

Crewe took the dog out. He looked discomfited, and when he came back apologized for the cramped quarters.

"Cramped quarters! Crewe, that's what we're doing to the house."

"Yes, sir."

"Crewe," said Peter, "England is a small nation. We manage better when we know that. Never more than seventy-five miles from the sea. Remember that. The sea is our iron fence. Remember Nelson. A remarkably small man, and one of the greatest Englishmen we have ever owed our hearts to. Have you seen his underclothes, with the left-shoulder bullet hole through them, at the Greenwich Museum? The ones he was wearing when he was killed at Trafalgar? They look as if they were to be worn by someone of nine or ten."

"But if the ballroom is to become the size of a sixpence, where are the twins to have their twenty-first?" said Crewe.

The dog snuggled toward the gas fire, and Annabel said that converting to gas was probably a good idea. She is sometimes impossibly practical.

"Crewe," said Peter, "it isn't a sixpence any longer, because we've gone into Europe. The sixpence is lost. The ballroom reduced will be a perfectly good disco for them, I should think. There's no harm in reducing scale. It's a matter of adjusting the eyes."

# Seven O'Clock of a Strange Millennium
## and All's Well

DOUGLASS BAMBURGH, aged seventy-one, was sitting in a pub in Northumberland with his mistress of long standing. She, too, was seventy-one: long since married to a man named Corbridge, but in Douglass's mind a girl forever christened Jessie Shaughnessy. They were watching Bamburgh's infant grandson crawling on a rug in front of the pub's electric fire. Jessie was a small, alert woman whose head made a sort of pecking movement when she was listening. She had been one of the first women surgeons in the country.

"You should never have packed it in," said Bamburgh.

"What 'it'?"

"Surgery."

"Darling, we've talked about this."

"At this age, we've talked about everything." He gave the heavy sigh of a seven-year-old.

"We decided together that I should pack it in. We wanted to see each other as much as possible. Anyway, a woman couldn't get very far in those days, and the cottage hospital wasn't up to much, was it? I should have been at a teaching hospital. I wasn't seeing enough of the meat."

"I've never been able to get over the way the medical profession speaks."

"As far as that goes, what's the difference between us?"

She drank some of her beer, and he waited for the rest of the thought.

"Do finish," he said. "Between?"

"Between my saying 'meat' and your calling yourself 'a farming man' when you've taken a double first and are by no means a farmer at all, at all."

"Don't be daffy."

"Daffy?"

"And don't choke into your beer, Jessie. You must know the word. You do live here."

"Of course, but we're much too well heeled to talk like that, and much too old."

"I am a Northumbrian."

"You're like what they call the potential of North Sea oil, considering the money that's been pumped into your education."

"Are we having an argument?" said Bamburgh.

"No, I'm having an observation."

"I'll get us a sherry." But Bamburgh didn't move. "It's a misfortune to carry the same surname as a castle, like me."

His grandson, Mike, six and a half months old, was a Bamburgh too. But being the age he was, he bore no grudge.

"Darling, Bamburgh is simply what you're called," Jessie said to Douglass.

"*Named.* I must have been *named* at some stage in our family history. As I said, I don't relish carrying the same name as a castle. It's much too much of a carry-on having to spell it, and I don't like the association with turrets. I'm not some arrow hole." Douglass had the sort of face that seems to have eaten into itself, but that was because dentistry is poor in Northumberland. His mouth had caved in a little.

"Only a little," said Jessie to herself.

"What?"

"I was thinking about your face."

"Well, my face is my own, even if my name does primarily belong to a castle. Good grief, to be castellated." He ate a sausage. "Interesting, how that verb then sounded as if it had a double meaning."

"Sherry would be nice," said Jessie, holding the child up by his fingers, which closed around hers as if the baby were drowning. The impression was quieted as soon as he looked at the baby's face, which was eager and full of doings. He played with Jessie's jewelry and seemed to be about to speak, like an intelligent and watchful animal that appears merely to choose to be silent. Jessie said a few sentences to him. A cheery woman married with absorption to the aforesaid Corbridge, another farmer, rather insensible, she had also always had a fine time with Douglass.

"Two things," she said to Douglass when he came back with the sherries.

"Yes?" said Douglass. He had brought a lemonade for Mike, the baby, who seemed to have been given merriment by the company but was also, for the moment, taxed by staggering about with the support of Jessie's fingers.

"I was muttering away to myself. Saying that when a baby begins to walk, it must think itself to be in a strange millennium," said Jessie.

"Good Lord."

"What?"

"Well, 'millennium' is a long word."

"No longer than 'castellated.'"

"Perhaps we've both eaten the public library in our lifetime. Our joint lifetime." A car went by and the snow chains on it rattled. "Like the chinking of harness on Russian horses in winter, isn't it?"

"There was no need to say that. It was what I was thinking anyway."

"Everything I say so often is, these days. You said there were two things," said Douglass. "What was the other thing?"

"You do worry about your face caving in."

Douglass kicked the electric fire, a fire of fake logs lit by electricity and giving off a minimum of warmth, saying "Turn round" to the mechanism that should have been moving behind red plastic to give an illusion of flames. "Come on, flicker."

"Does your toe hurt when you do that?" said Jessie. The baby seemed troubled and sat down on the rug opposite the unconvivial fire.

"And what's the matter with him?" Douglass said, bawling a little, as he did when he was worried. Somebody on his farm had told him the night before that Mr. Corbridge had been asking questions about him and Jessie, questions about the matters that had always seemed settled. Some derangement in the offing, to be quelled. The long arm of blight, he thought. And it would be a blight, he surprised himself by thinking, if the blessed Mr. Corbridge—politely, that "Mr."—were not to be with us. You don't shift ballast without rocking boats. Besides, we're fond of him, and what if he's afraid?

"You can't go on learning to walk for hours at a stretch, can you?" said Jessie of Mike. "And he may have been concerned about your toe, of course, though that's something we'll never be sure of, like many another thing."

"I'm fine, thank you, beautiful girl."

Jessie looked down at her glass, or perhaps at the baby. Both, probably. "I'm not beautiful or a girl any longer, but good of you to go on saying so."

He kissed her with sweetness, cupping her face in his hands as though it were a glass raised in a toast and he about to drink from it, and then said, "As to me, darling, what was your second point again?"

"Your teeth."

"It isn't the teeth, it's the lack of teeth."

"I always said you should have been a philosopher."

"Meaning I'm too well read to farm."

"I daresay it all comes from thinking."

"Nothing to debar a farming man from thinking. Some of

the best thoughts in England's history have come from Northumberland. Now, this bleeding dentist, you see."

"You say you're bleeding?"

"No, darling, your hearing's going. We'll traipse off to the ear, nose, and throat department in Hexham when we go to the library. God rot."

"I'm not keen on it when you swear."

"Blimey, when we chose to rough it so long ago. No Lady Margaret Hall here."

"Who?"

Douglass said the Oxford college's name again more slowly and she apologized. He picked up the baby and then put him down, because he was struggling.

"Picking him up would sometimes be an offense when he's learning to walk, and soon to talk," he said to Jessie. "Won't be long," he said to Mike with care, and then, to Jessie, "This tooth that came out, the one you haven't noticed—"

"I did, darling. That's why I asked—"

"—it's more than a tooth to me, because it involves my face. Well, yes, I suppose you realize that or you wouldn't have come into Newcastle with me."

"The tooth seemed all right last week. You didn't tell me anything more."

"You were with your husband until today."

"But we've always managed, haven't we? And, to get back to the tooth—"

"As I said, it came out. Over the weekend. The dentist in Newcastle was away for the weekend. I reached him. He told me to try putting it back with chewing gum until Monday. I said chewing gum would never pass my lips. He advised bubble gum, and when I said I'd never heard of it he said that as a dentist he was commending it. So I went into Newcastle to get some. Bubble gum."

Jessie picked up the baby. "On your own."

"Well, you can't stalk into a *pub* in remotest Northumberland and expect to get bubble gum. Sausages yes, bubble gum no. So I went into Newcastle, with the chains on my car, and found the stuff. It's off prescription. But it didn't work. I was having a piece of toast and the tooth came out again. Waste of petrol. The dentist, I telephoned him—"

"All the way in the snow to the telephone box—"

"—the dentist said it was because of the hostile environment of the mouth. Fancy having a part of your own anatomy fighting you. As if there weren't enough threats. Your husband, for instance. I love you very much."

"You talk as if I were already gone. Not gone. Not done."

Jessie took him back to her house, her husband being away in Leeds—away as he had been so often in their forty-five years of marriage, inciting disturbance, displaying complaisance—and they watched black-and-white television together on the sofa, with the baby comfortably asleep between them. The television reception was bad, because of the weather and the age of the set, but they happened on a welcome replay of an interview with a bearded young man sitting at the head of the queue at Wimbledon that past summer for the men's-singles final. The young man had been there, he said, for five days. He had food, a sleeping bag, and two placid, panting sheepdogs with him. As he fed ice cream and water to the dogs, he told the interviewer that he wasn't really much interested in tennis. "It's the queueing I like. It's the occasion."

Douglass and Jessie watched, with care. They had seen the program before. Douglass said, without turning around, "You might almost have arranged it for me. I think *this* counts as an occasion, wouldn't you say?" He didn't customarily go so far. He kissed Jessie, and then went away into another room as if claustrophobic. He came back saying, "I know your husband's going to punish us, and the terrible thing is that he had exactitude on his side morally, though not emotionally. Probably. I wonder if he has any conception, any conception whatever, of what we mean to each other. I beg your pardon, Jessie. I seem to have put my sense of humor somewhere and I can't find it."

"You have it in saying you've lost it." She kissed him, and he carried away his grandchild.

A WEEK later, Jessie kept repeating a phrase to herself about being in the midst of life. It seemed not a bad place to be, on the whole, though the present actualities were hard. The snow was pelting down. The car chains were chinking. A young policeman, who had come in a car with snow chains that chinked with a blitheness at odds with authority, was in her drawing room to question her.

"And this farm poison," said the policeman. His rubber mackintosh was visibly a nuisance to him, but he was too raw, too official, too cold to take it off. Jessie sat him beside the range and gave him some stock.

"My friend, Mr. Bamburgh, must have thought my husband was going to put an end to us. To Douglass and me."

"Murder?"

"No, not in the sense of killing us."

"In what sense?"

"Of putting his foot down, don't you see. Of stopping our seeing each other."

"A *crime passionnel*. But it was Mr. Bamburgh's farm poison."

"Officer, is the stock too hot?"

"Quite cool, Madam, but we don't imbibe on the job. You'd better tell me the story in your own words."

"Well, I haven't anybody else's words, have I? As I understand it, Mr. Bamburgh was fearful that my husband was going to put an end to our friendship. So he apparently, without my knowing it, injected a dose of farm poison into my husband's bottle of rum in the Flemish cupboard over there. So my husband must have drunk a little, being a very tired—a most hardworking man, and I was out—and he got acute pains in his stomach, and when I came back I thought he was so unwell that it was best for me to drive him to hospital rather than wait for the ambulance to Newcastle."

"Twenty-three miles?"

"Twenty-two by the back roads."

"And the hospital records show an attempt to murder you."

"No, no. When I got back from hospital, with my husband quite better, I did something I don't usually do. I'm not a drinker. But to relieve the loneliness—"

"You didn't telephone Mr. Bamburgh?"

"It would have been horribly inapt, don't you know. One is on one's own in such matters. But I'm afraid I had recourse to my husband's bottle of rum, and I too had quite a lot of misery for so falling into mischief. It was to relieve the tension, of course, but an infantile method. I had to lie down on the floor but got to a telephone to ring a most thoughtful neighbor to ask her to take me to hospital. She arranged with me to stay here to save the cat from being lonely. Now, you're not to be concerned about cruelty, because there has been mind on all sides. But when my friend got back from hospital she took a little of the rum, again to relieve the tension, and it seems that she also got horrible stomach pains and of course had to ask for an ambulance. And there was also the worry about the cat. Pelion on Ossa, you see."

"An intent to murder the neighbor, as well as your husband and yourself?"

"Oh no. No on all counts. Everyone survived. My husband and Mr. Bamburgh together got in a social-services woman to look after the cat. While we were away."

"The cat seems to have been major." The policeman rustled in his mackintosh. "According to your account of the crime or crimes."

"*Preëminent*, to an extent. Loneliness can't be ignored, can it? Isolation being another matter, because often chosen."

The policeman was cold enough to drink some of the stock, which strengthened his resolve. "And to go back to the crime or crimes."

"Well, officer, everyone survived, as I said. But it is always possible, of course, that ills may have been dealt out."

"To the cat?"

"We got a bill for eight pounds thirty from the social-services woman for cat food and litter. My husband and Mr. Bamburgh split the cost. Both being fond of the cat, don't you see. And I stumped up two quid."

"Giving it to which party?"

"To my husband."

"This question of the ills you were speaking of, Mrs. Corbridge. The stomach incidents?"

"No."

"As I thought."

"I was thinking of damage."

"You mean homicide. Intention to do grievous bodily harm." The young officer's pencil dropped and he didn't do anything about it, but instead finished his stock.

"You've dropped your pencil," said Jessie, picking it up.

"Thank you."

"There was no bodily harm, officer. We have long since reached an accommodation, theologically speaking."

"Would you like a tape recorder? We could give you a transcript. I don't take shorthand."

"Well, it's a dying art, isn't it? No, there's no call for a transcript. I know what I'm saying."

"Accommodation, you were carrying on about."

"Theological accommodation, officer. I was thinking, have often thought, that there is always the possibility that theology may be wrong. I mean that injury may be done in the process of accommodation, which is then apparently comic and seems well understood by all the people involved. But as far as the ills we're speaking of go, they can't be accounted for by hospital folders, can they? In the chaos of records, we may have lost sight of mercy."